GODDESS
OF FILTH

GODDESS OF FILTH

V. CASTRO

Creature Publishing
Brooklyn, NY

ISBN 978-1-951971-03-8
LCCN 2020946639

Cover design by Luísa Dias
Spine illustration by Rachel Kelli

CREATUREHORROR.COM

 @creaturelit

@creaturepublishing

Dedicated to all the women finding their way.
You are not alone.

GODDESS
OF FILTH

Chapter 1

"I only found ones with saints or Jesus on them. You think they will scare the spirits away?"

Fernanda rolled her eyes, snatching the candles from Ana to light them. "It's just a little fun. Besides, it's my damn early birthday after all, and the last one I'll spend with you pendejas for a while." Fernanda was leaving, and soon. This Saturday night we celebrated the birthday we would miss once she left for college.

I took my place on the floor next to Fernanda and Ana, and Perla handed me a glass of a fizzing brown concoction I hoped would be strong. By the looks of the half-empty glasses and open cans, the others had started already. I took two big refreshing alcoholic gulps of Southern Comfort and Coke, nasty shit only good for getting fucked up. The ice felt good in my mouth, even if it made my teeth ache. My empty stomach chewed on the booze, sending a sense of relaxation through my body. Five of us sat in a circle doing our best to emulate the girls in *The Craft*, hoping to unleash some power to take us all away from our home to the place of our dreams. But we weren't witches. We were five Chicanas living in San Antonio, Texas, one year out of high school.

"So, who is doing the honors of calling on the universe to find a ghost or demon to talk to?" Pauline chugged the last of her Modelo.

We exchanged glances in an alcohol-induced haze.

Fuck it, it would be me leading this séance. I'd do it as a leaving present to Fernanda, since not a dime from my fortnightly paycheck could be spared for a gift she could take with her.

I made eye contact with my four friends, letting them know I was serious.

"All right, hold hands and don't let go. I want you to believe in your hearts we can be heard." What I meant was, I need to be heard because my thoughts barely carried over the pop of the deep fat fryer during a double shift. I was sick of feeling like splattered grease stuck on the wall.

Fernanda giggled at my sudden onset of clairvoyance. She always said I was so fucking dramatic. *Yes, bitch, I am!* was my response. When your insides are egg white soft, you learn to develop an exterior tougher than fossilized dead things.

I first became aware of this fact with a boy by the name of Tip Top; he was a Mexican wannabe member of the '90s group Kris Kross with his oversized polos and Dickies too baggy for his spindly limbs. He parted his hair in the center and applied so much gel it crunched to the touch. We stood facing each other, arguing the way adults would. He kept pressing me to hold his hand when I didn't want to. Pressing me to fool around when I didn't feel ready. "You hate me so much, so just go on and hit me. I dare you," I sneered, taking a step closer to him with my fists balled at my sides, ready to receive a blow I'm not sure why I felt I deserved. I shook inside, wanting to run and hide.

He glared at me. "Nah, you ain't worth it."

I raised my chin in defiance, hoping the tears on the verge of falling would roll back into my eyes. They did. The following day most of the cliques heard about the fight.

"You're a hard bitch. I heard about your shenanigans, acting all angry. That's not pretty you know," one of the cool boys whispered in passing, also wearing an oversized polo and strong Drakkar cologne. I couldn't tell everyone, *I'm really not.*

"Okay, Lourdes. Give us your best dramatics and call something." Fernanda chuckled.

That second beer had made it to her head. Good, she would be nice and tipsy for a cheap scare. I thought about who I wanted to contact. If I could reach a spirit, it would have to be a thing of power, something to give me hope.

I concentrated every ounce of will, the kind of ganas you would need in a life or death situation, then released it all through my lips with authority.

"I want to reach a spirit. An old spirit, one from before the world was what we know today. If you are there, speak to us. Give us a sign."

Ana, Perla, Pauline, and Fernanda had their eyes closed. Not me. If there was something or someone listening, I had to see it. I was as broke in faith as I was in pocket. This was a time when you had ICE storming around like possessed Storm Troopers on crack, people getting shot trying to learn or pray or buy milk. Stories of people going missing. Bodies of displaced people washed up on river beds and coastlines for all to see, to cry about, but ultimately forget. You've heard of the Cold War? This was the beginning of the Border Wars. I wondered how much time was really left for any of us. I think I would have settled for the devil himself if he promised me things would work out in the end—for me, for my friends, for my sisters who couldn't even spell their names yet.

It was quiet when the candles flickered from an unseen breath, illuminating the sacred heart of Jesus and La Virgen with a glow that seemed too bright for cheap wax in glass from the supermarket. I had never seen a flame burn through a candle so quickly. The remnants were like those sad photos of collapsing icebergs. Flames belly danced across the room and over our bodies.

The words were a mumble, barely audible, but there. Fernanda released my sweaty grip. She unfolded her legs to adopt a squatting position. Both her arms extended to the ceiling as if she held onto a branch, readying her body for birth in the wild. Her chanting increased in volume as she stared at nothing, her wide eyes reflecting the flames. In the darkness, it appeared as if the fire was inside her skull. The rest of the circle watched in fear as a husky breathless voice filled the room, sounding less and less like Fernanda's.

"Stop it, Fernanda! That isn't funny!" shouted Pauline, trying to avoid looking between Fernanda's legs as her skirt hitched up to reveal bloodstained panties. Our cycles were always in sync, and it wasn't time. Cramps that usually signalled the beginning of my period caused me to wince in pain and clutch my belly. I looked around to see if this was just me. I couldn't tell through the expressions of terror on their faces.

Perla crept over to Fernanda and gave her a gentle shove, trying to topple her over. I hoped Fernanda would burst into laughter, that the joke was on us. But she was not the joking type. Fernanda's feet remained firmly planted on the ground, arms still spread to the atmosphere, blood dripping from between her legs like rainwater falling from a leaf.

Ana recoiled to the far side of my room against the window with the Jesus-printed candle. "My mother said no one can hear you when the devil is near. Is she possessed? We shouldn't have done this!"

Fernanda dropped to her hands and knees. The sound of the slap against the tiles made us all jump. She moaned, grunted, and hissed. Then silence, and she raised her head to look at us. The expression on her face through parted hair was ecstasy and pain. Her lips became thinner, her teeth larger, as she opened her mouth like a bottomless, black cenote. She spoke again, only louder this time so we could hear.

"Naqui.Naqui.Naqui.　　Niyoli.Niyoli.Niyoli." Her eyeballs shook with sporadic tremors, her pupils those of someone rolling on ecstasy. I was closest to her and probably the only one to notice that they were changing in shape and color. Suddenly the air-conditioning was too cold on my skin. There was no way I could be seeing what I was seeing.

Pauline's voice cracked in panic as she stammered. "Is she speaking Latin . . . or, or Aramaic? Like, you know, in the movies. The language of Jesus."

"It's not fucking Aramaic," I snapped as I shot her a mean, uncalled-for look. I moved closer to Fernanda to get a better understanding of what she was saying. She would never hurt me. It was another language, and it was old, yet still spoken. It was Nahuatl. I knew because I had seen a documentary about the indigenous people of Mexico in AP History. When I could afford classes at the community college, I wanted to study history, my history. As much pride as I took in my mestiza roots, I knew very little of it. Another source of anger for me, as if I needed more.

"Make her stop, Lourdes!" cried Perla, curling her arms tightly around Pauline and Ana. They were huddled together looking at me for answers. I was never top of the class or best dressed, but I always knew how to take control.

Fernanda crawled toward us like a creature without a face, her hair now fallen over the top half of her body which moved in a contorted, disjointed manner. Umbilical cord-length, black streaks ran down her legs, dripping onto the tiles of my bedroom floor. Ana, Perla, and Pauline were crying and screaming, clutching the candle with La Virgen like it would save them.

I ran to the door and flipped on the light switch. The candles extinguished on their own, and Fernanda collapsed. Her body looked like a discarded, crumpled piece of clothing. Ana screamed at the sight of blood smeared across the floor and across our friend's face. The air had the faint scent of sea mist and extinguished flames.

"Is she dead? Oh my God! Lourdes! Do something!"

Perla and Pauline looked around the room in desperation, their bodies trembling, not knowing what to do. I knew none of us wanted to tell our parents there was trouble because we had stolen beer and booze from all our homes. Most of our parents wouldn't care, but Fernanda's mother would have a fit of apocalypse-telenovela dramatics, probably banning us from seeing her daughter until she left for college. I bent down to place my head against her chest and a hand over her nose. The rhythm of breathing and beating seemed normal.

"She's just out cold." A slight sense of relief eased the tension on their faces. Ana helped me lay Fernanda in a comfortable position on the floor with a pillow beneath her head.

"What do we do now, Lourdes?" Ana whimpered.

We all looked down at our friend. The last thing I needed was questions and wailing. I got enough of that with my little sisters.

"I want you all to go home. Let me stay. If nothing changes by sunrise, I'll call an ambulance."

"What? Why? We can't leave you alone," said Pauline.

"Why not? There's nothing you can do. If something is wrong, better one of us in trouble than all of us."

"I don't like it." Perla shook her head, fighting back tears.

"No offense, Perla, but this is why. Don't go crying. It will be fine."

Pauline pulled her lips into a tight knot and bent down to touch Fernanda's forehead with a shaky palm. She moved to Fernanda's chest, watching her hand rise and fall.

"She is right. We all know Fernanda. She might be embarrassed if we make a fuss over her when this turns out to be nothing. Just an emotional outburst." Pauline stood up again to face me. "If something is wrong you better call us immediately and tell the authorities the truth. We are in this together. Okay?"

"Understood. Don't any of you worry. It's a bad period and a lot of emotions."

"Let me help you clean up."

"Don't worry about it, Ana. It will give me something to do while I wait."

We hugged each other goodbye, and I got to work. I cleaned the blood from Fernanda's legs, placing a towel between them to soak up the flow. On my hands and knees, I scrubbed the floor with paper towels. As I wiped the same damn spot for over an hour, I tried to come up with what I would say. What explanation could I give for the events that proceeded our friend falling unconscious? We didn't do anything wrong. We were just a couple of friends being ourselves. Being a young woman isn't a crime. This wasn't Salem. But at the same time, I knew this wouldn't be let go. It's about how visible your veins are beneath your skin and what hangs between your legs. If I didn't feel absolutely fucked before, I did now.

I sat on the floor with Fernanda, trying to make sense of her behavior. She wasn't a wild girl, not like me. My purse was filled with condoms, and I didn't like children very much, besides my sisters. She had morals and a soft heart. I leaned my head and neck against the mattress. All I could do was wait for her to open her eyes. She had to wake up.

◈◈

Almost a year earlier to the day, we had sat in a semi-circle of plastic lawn chairs in Ana's backyard celebrating graduation. The aroma of beef fat sizzling on hot coals and charred chicken skin filled the air. I flopped my aching legs and back into the hard chair, using my feet to take off my work shoes. I changed into chanclas stashed in my bag.

"Fuck, I can't do this forever. How was the ceremony?"

Pauline threw me a wet Mike's Hard Lemonade from a blue cooler filled with beer and bottled mixed drinks. "You just need to find your passion, or something you don't mind doing for a while. I'm not exactly passionate about braces or dentistry, but every time I sell something the boss promises to give me a little extra. It's just for a hot minute until I figure it all out." She took a drink of Modelo. "Oh, and you didn't miss anything."

I opened the bottle and gulped it down to quench my thirst, thinking if only it was as easy as that. My thirst was beyond alcohol and water, a burning that wouldn't be satiated. I appreciated the lie Pauline told me with regards to the ceremony. The lemon felt sour and I didn't want to finish it. I knew my passion.

Pauline slid back into her seat, bopping her head to the TLC CD her brother Ruben had put in the boombox. She was a good friend with the power to convince anyone of anything. Just before graduation, she got me out of detention with only her words. I had missed a homework assignment. When the teacher asked me to stay behind, Pauline stood shoulder to shoulder right next to me. She sucked her teeth and folded her arms across her body.

"C'mon, Miss. Do you know Lourdes works almost a full-time job for extra money? She has three younger sisters she takes care of, too. So she forgot *one* assignment." Pauline shrugged.

When we left the classroom, I gave Pauline a hug. Senior year was hard, knowing there was nothing happening after. I had to stay behind because I couldn't even afford community yet. My parents didn't earn enough to put extra aside for me with three other mouths to feed, or have any collateral for a loan. They also did not fall below the poverty line to qualify me for free money. But I appreciated Pauline's support at that moment.

"Girl, you have the devil's tongue. You could probably sell the motherfucker fire."

She pulled away and gave me a wink. "It just takes a little bruja magic."

Pauline could not talk away my feelings of frustration, or my anger for missing graduation. Next to us, Fernanda drank Sprite, sulking she missed making valedictorian by only a few points. She was leaving for college in the fall on an academic scholarship to a fancy school in Philadelphia that the President's daughter had attended.

We were all sure she would forget about us in the chaos of exams, essays, and internships that would carry her even further away.

Fernanda got my attention in middle school when a rubber band popped off her braces in math class and landed in the middle of my desk. I could tell she thought I would give her a dirty look as she blushed in embarrassment, on the verge of tears. Instead, I handed it back to her. Thanks to Fernanda, I passed math.

"Pauline is right. You didn't miss anything." There was a hint of bitterness in her voice. Her eyes flicked towards Ruben when he brought over a bag of Cheetos, a faint blush blooming on her cheeks. She immediately looked down at her drink.

"I thought your speech was wonderful, Fernanda. Salutatorian is still a great honor."

Her eyes moved to his shoes. "Thanks, Ruben. Um . . . do you think you can give me a ride home later, since you're the only one not drinking?"

"Of course. Just tell me when you're ready to leave."

"My parents asked about you," piped Ana, seeing the grumpy disposition I was trying to hold in. "I'm still on the fence about a teaching assistant position, but if you are interested my parents could probably hook you up."

Ana was from a family of teachers but was unsure if she wanted to pursue teaching herself. However, whether she liked it or not, she could explain the most complex ideas in simple terms and possessed an open kindness that drew people in, especially children.

"Thanks, girl. I'll think about it." I took my sandals off to feel the freshly cut grass between my toes. "How's your mom liking her new position as superintendent?"

"Young ladies! Congratulations on this very important time in your life when you move from one world to another. I lit candles for all of you at the feet of La Virgen before coming here."

I looked behind me to see Father Moreno, the local priest, standing there. I had nothing against him, just what he stood for.

"Thank you," we all mumbled as a courtesy. None of us were religious, although our families were. We didn't really know him. I shifted in my seat, hoping he would move on from our little group. This was supposed to be a party, despite my mood like a tepid Mike's Hard Lemonade. Then Ruben saved us.

"Glad you could make it, Father Moreno."

"Ah, an important man. May God bless you for your service. You must tell me all about your new position overseas! I cannot tell you what a blessing it was to serve as chaplain on your base. Do you have a moment?"

Ruben, the polite type that mothers loved, looked disappointed as he glanced towards the empty seat between Fernanda and Perla, then back at the priest.

"Yes, sir. It will be quite an adventure."

"Fantastic. Is that your father's chicken I smell?"

"Yes, sir. Why don't we go fix you a plate?"

I was relieved when they walked towards the card table topped with aluminium trays filled with mounds of food and two buckets of sweet tea from Bill Miller.

Perla wiggled in her chair to a cumbia. Perla and I had become friends when a boy she liked expressed interest in me. I couldn't speak Spanish, and he was a student from Mexico. Cesar with his slicked back hair, oversized jeans, and NBA jerseys over a T-shirt. His voice so quiet I could barely understand what he said. He was self-conscious trying to hide his Spanglish, hide that he went to special classes to help him to read and speak English. Perla understood him loud and clear. If Perla had a power, it would be languages. She spoke English, Spanish, aced French, and could have had an A in Latin if she didn't get so bored with it. A language for old men she called it. I gave her my blessing to date him or fuck him. She did both, recounting all the dirty details to us on a Monday. It almost deepened my resentment that we didn't speak Spanish at home. We sat in a circle giving the term oral tradition a new meaning. Sometimes when I was alone, I would think about her salacious stories with Cesar.

"I wish Cesar was here," she said, "I wanna dance! You are all too serious. We graduated! Can we party?"

That was a year ago, the day I missed high school graduation. My family didn't care enough to ask about the details before, and if they did, it would have meant paying for the extras that go along with the ceremony. Anyway, it was just another piece of paper, like a birth certificate or a passport to show your place in the world. Deep down I was envious of Fernanda, but if one of us could make it big, that would be everything. Someone had to show us there were opportunities available for barrio girls. I mean, we would never be mistaken for blue bloods because our skin is the shade of brown that camouflages veins. Perla, another one on the honor roll in our school, was in the same situation as me. Being smart is great, but there are a lot of smart people out there. Everybody wants to be somebody, but that shit has a price tag and there is no way to cut corners, not for us. That is why Ruben enrolled in the military after doing so well in JROTC in high school.

👁👁

I felt myself nodding off. I didn't know if it was a dream or if it was real, but the sound of clicking against tiles made my lolling head jerk upright. I looked around the bright room to see where the noise was coming from.

It couldn't be my sisters because they were all in Lake Jackson visiting family. We had no pets or problems with mice.

The scratching persisted, followed by a low hiss similar to the sound Fernanda had made earlier that night. I couldn't identify the direction it was coming from until it was right next to me. Four hands, two on either side of my hips and two scuttling towards Fernanda like spider legs. Fingertips as black as frostbitten appendages twitched in exploration. My innards felt like pop rocks crackling and jumping towards my mouth. Before I could move, they caught hold of us, folding our bodies neatly in half and pulling us beneath the bed. I could feel my organs and bones being crushed to powder the deeper I sank. Fernanda remained unconscious, a blanket of floppy hair and skin. I couldn't shout for help because my lungs were crushed flat.

My head jerked again, and I awoke in the same position I'd been in before falling asleep. Rods of sunlight brightened the room as Fernanda opened her eyes, smacking her mouth as if all the moisture had been sucked out. Her lips appeared dried and cracked. I scrambled to my knees.

"Fernanda! You're all right." I wanted to thank those sainted candles for this miracle.

"Lourdes? What happened?"

Another face looking for answers I didn't have. My relief deflated a little. I'd hoped she would tell me.

"What do you remember?"

She lifted herself to a sitting position next to me. "It was like a nightmare. Everything was on fire and filthy, including myself. I was in the mud barefoot with my legs and hands covered in dirt. And the heat . . . my God, the heat."

"You scared the girls real bad. You were in some sort of trance, spoke in Nahuatl and started your period." She looked between her legs at the hand towel blotched in red. "Sorry, I had to improvise."

Without making an expression or sound she buried her head between my armpit and breast to cry, bringing her legs closer to mine. The sobs shook her entire body.

I wasn't sure how to react. The moment to act was over and now shock had settled in. I had only a small sense of belief in the supernatural, which came from a basic human desire to know what else was out there. Since the age of eleven I had walked in and out of Pentecostal and Baptist churches because my stepfather was Baptist. Saw my mother "saved" as I sat in the front pew of a church that could seat about a hundred people. She wore a white cotton robe as the preacher dunked her in a pool of warm water behind the pulpit. A declaration that Jesus ruled her heart. Reluctantly, I went ahead with the same ceremony at twelve to stop her pestering me about my salvation. Nothing changed inside of me when I emerged from the water.

Voices cried out, bodies swayed, bands played in jubilation to conjure the descending dove, the power of God. Despite the noise and great sense of belief surrounding me, I still felt nothing; only once was there enough guilt for me to think about tossing out my Danzig CD with the black demon on the front that made me think about sex.

"Purity in mind and purity in heart! You are for your husband and Christ and no one else," was the preacher's mantra. Every Wednesday. Every fucking Wednesday—who goes to church on a Wednesday?—I watched my mother who couldn't carry a note sing happily in the church choir because her man was happy she bounced around up there. I glowered at the sight and sound. It seemed so inauthentic. I stroked Fernanda's hair as she continued to sob.

There had to be a logical explanation like Pauline said. I squeezed my eyes shut to remember every moment that had led up to this point. No way did I see what I saw. No, I would push it all down. *Think, Lourdes. THINK!* I knew Fernanda worried endlessly about how her parents would afford all the extras of university over four years.

She had to be the second to graduate in the family. Was this some sort of breakdown before college with all the pressure she felt to succeed? When you come from a family of immigrants, showing your validity, possessing papers, was essential. In some ways I felt lucky no one expected anything of me. The only one who cared if I was a failure or not was myself.

I had to cheer her up.

"Hey, this was a Saturday night you will never forget. Don't worry. Remember the time when we were at the water park at thirteen and I started my period? My legs were pink, and I blamed it on melted raspa. All those boys were there . . . Come on, we need to get you home before breakfast so your mom doesn't freak out. And you need something for that."

I managed to make her laugh as she wiped her tears, but something was whispering behind her eyes. Her pupils still trembled. She appeared confused as she looked around the hallway to find the bathroom, even though we'd spent hours together hanging out at my house.

"Fernanda, it's just to the right and tampons in the bottom cabinet."

"Thanks. I'm fine. Just dizzy from being hungry. I hardly ate yesterday filling out all these work study applications. Maybe some food after—a bean and cheese breakfast taco or a honey chicken biscuit from Whataburger."

"Yeah, sure. Whatever you need."

She closed the bathroom door, and I sent the girls a message.

Everything will be ok. Fernanda is up and hungry!

I grabbed my bag and shoes to leave. We drove in silence to the 24-hour Taco Cabana to get her food and then straight to her home. The tacos aren't the best, but they'll do when you are in a bind. She ate next to me without saying a word, chewing slowly. Fernanda usually gobbled junk food, as her mother despised the stuff.

When we arrived at her house, I told Fernanda to call me later. Before she stepped out of the car, she opened her mouth to speak with eyes that were her own, puffy from crying. They reminded me of an unsettled sky holding the heaviness of rain that refused to fall. "Thanks."

I didn't want to upset her before seeing her mother, so I didn't push. She never called that day.

"Can you please stop checking your phone and help me?" my mother asked, exasperated with dark circles beneath her eyes, the creases around her mouth and eyes sagging downward in a permanent frown. I wanted to scream, "If you are not happy, say something dammit!" But we are not allowed to say those things in the event that we sound ungrateful.

My stepfather would leave for days at a time with the railroad, leaving the burden of housework and child rearing to us. When he was around, his time was spent cutting the expansive lawn or clearing dead wood from the trees. I looked at two piles of laundry that needed folding and back to the groceries my mother had already hauled onto the kitchen floor. My sisters attacked the contents like gremlins eating past midnight. Where would I begin? I shooed the little ones away to put away the cold contents. My only day off would be filled with more work.

"What are you making for lunch?" my sister Rosalie asked. I huffed and gave her a weak smile.

"Whatever you want as long as it's grilled cheese."

My mother walked in, kicking the door closed behind her as she carried in the last paper bags of groceries. "Why don't you make lunch for everyone and a little of something else that can be eaten for dinner?" I did as I was told, wanting to say no and look for opportunities for myself. It would have to wait. I pushed it down, like eating cold leftovers.

Chapter 2

Fernanda opened the door as quietly as she could. Her mother slept light. She slipped off her flats while closing the door and held the handle until it locked without the click.

Taking her steps from heel to the ball of her foot she crept into her room, closing the door soundlessly. She had no energy for anything except crawling into bed. There was a ringing in her head, a spinning like the first time she got drunk with Lourdes. As she lay there with her eyes closed the spinning continued, like a vortex of water draining loudly until that sound morphed into a woman's voice speaking a language she didn't comprehend. The languages continued to change, like her brain was flipping between radio stations. Some of the languages she recognized, until it was clear.

Fernanda. Can you understand me now?

Fernanda's eyes snapped open. Who or what was talking within her head? She whispered, "yes."

I have traveled a long way. I am here after being drawn to your collective anger and strength, each different in spirit but the same in their power to reverberate.

"I can't remember what happened tonight. Just a nightmare. Am I going crazy?" Tears streamed from the corners of Fernanda's eyes. The feeling of having no control over her mind, the source of her pride, made her want to punch and kick the walls of her room. Hearing voices? Was she on the verge of losing it?

You're not crazy. I will show you many things, if you want me to.

"You are real? No way. If I'm not crazy, show yourself in the flesh. Not like the saints my mother prays to. What are you?" Fernanda sat upright in bed looking around in a panic, hoping to see something. It was hard to believe she wasn't going insane.

I am very real. I am female, just like you. Look in your mirror.

Fernanda scooted to the edge of her bed, realizing the dizziness from before had vanished.

She slowly bent her body to the left to look into her armoire mirror. She saw her own reflection. Fernanda stepped off the bed and walked closer to her image. Morning light filtered into her room. She blinked. As she drew closer to the mirror, she could see her eyes were not her own.

"Oh my god. Oh my god! What happened to me?" Fernanda stood gripped in terror seeing the terrible transformation of her eyes into black narrow slits. They now resembled those of a creature.

Shhhh. Don't worry. Look closer and inside you will see me.

Fernanda leaned so close her nose nearly touched the mirror. There, in the center of her pupils, a woman glowed like a firefly. Beautiful. Maybe a fairy? No, that wasn't right. The voice was stronger than that. This was no Tinkerbell. Fernanda's fear turned to fascination.

"Why are you inside of me?"

For many reasons. I have always had an affinity for humans, for your bodies, and this world needs hope. The ages of building great pyramids, like in my adopted home of Mexico, have long been over. I want to rebuild something new that can be carried in your hand, but as everlasting as those structures.

"I want to do great things, too. It feels overwhelming at times. I don't know what to expect or if I am even good enough."

You are good enough. In all cultures there are those that work as conduits, healers, shaman, witches . . . so many names. Some are more tolerant of those reaching to the other side while others believe it is an act of evil. As if they alone possess such absolute knowledge, something they can hoard and deal out as they see fit. I am a goddess and you a mortal female with much to learn about life and about yourself. However, these are the very attributes that will allow me to thrive without harming you. At first it will be like you experienced before; I will need control for a time as we test our compatibility. Perhaps we can do great things together?

Fernanda continued to stare in wonder at her own eyes. "I like that idea."

🍂🍂

When I went to check on Fernanda on my way to work the following morning, she sat outside in her mother's flower bed of prized roses, now wilted from the heat. Fernanda's hair lay limp, parted in the center against her face and shoulders. Her lips, usually bare, were slicked with black lipstick and her eyes were heavily outlined, winged at the sides like I taught her, the way my mother hated because it made me look like a Pachuca. But the makeup was just the first of the oddities. She wore only white cotton panties and a cotton T-shirt. She squatted in a birthing position in the dirt, crimson stains between her legs in full view. Her mother knelt before her, red-faced and sweating, strands of wet hair curled around her neck. She pleaded in Spanish for her to come into the house. Cars slowed down as they passed. Fernanda mumbled to herself in Nahuatl, not even glancing in my direction when I approached.

Mrs. Garcia whipped her head towards me with a look that could have been a lashing from a cat-o'-nine-tails.

"What have you girls been teaching my daughter? Is she on the drugs? The alcohol? I know you probably have secret boyfriends. There is no one to control you in that mess you call a family!"

I wanted to curse her out on the spot, slap her hard. But it wouldn't help Fernanda. "Nothing! She isn't on anything. We only played a game."

Mrs. Garcia gasped, placing one hand over her mouth and the other over the crucifix around her neck. "El Diablo! You have been playing with El Diablo! Haven't you?! Now he has taken her because of her purity. You might not be innocent, but my daughter is. Leave!"

My cheeks went hot and my fist balled. Just like the time in middle school when I was blamed for a game of truth or dare. I sat in front of my mother and stepfather as they recounted the other parents' accusations. It was all my idea. I was the corruptor. Was I already having sex? Smoking? Knowing nothing I could say or do would make anyone less mad, I stayed silent and took the blame for the schoolyard game. I carried our sin for being curious prepubescent kids. Fuck her. I walked away because if I dug my heels in, I would be late for my shift.

I couldn't sleep thinking about Fernanda. My texts went unanswered, as did my phone calls to her home landline. The girls had as much luck as me trying to contact her, and they were getting freaked out.

I thought everything was fine when you left her? messaged Pauline.

I did too. I don't know what is happening. Keep trying. I wrote back.

We decided to give it another week before we all showed up at her front door. Pauline, the young woman with the silver tongue, would knock first. Mrs. Garcia had the demeanor of a bloody bull being prodded in a ring. She had no problem calling everyone's parents to give them an earful for at least half an hour. No one wanted to be on the other end of that conversation or be marked in her bad books. Even Mr. Garcia got ribbed regularly for holding his tongue around his wife, sheepishly replying, "*She* is the boss."

When I slept, I dreamed about a naked woman climbing out of a cenote with thick lips smeared with black and eyes of an ancient beast, a caiman. Double lids blinked over horizontal pupils rolling in every direction, inspecting her surroundings. As they moved, the light reflected off flecks of gold in her irises. Water rolled off her body as steam floated into the air in gossamer wisps. Black hair heavy with water lay flat against her scalp, accentuating high cheek bones on a square, wide face. When she opened her mouth, an elongated tongue covered in raised bumps licked the ground. The tip struck hard, leaving red and blue flames in its wake. The woman took the same stance as Fernanda, bleeding between her legs, pleading to the sky in Nahuatl with eyes facing the back of her head. When she spoke, her open mouth showed teeth worn from gnashing. In her nudity I could see the tips of her nipples glistening with white milky stars made of hot gas. Her skin was the same dark brown as my own, but she seemed to burn from the inside like a human candle.

Everything about her could be considered a nightmare, but I wasn't scared. She glowed with fury, beauty, and power. Half woman, half beast, this was no ghost or demon. She was everything I wished I could be. Fire and anger with bitterness wet my lips. My soul wanted to fall to its knees and beg her to tell me her secrets. When she became aware of my presence, turning that caiman gaze straight at me, I awoke startled and sweating, as if I had slept next to a bonfire.

I persisted in my calls to Fernanda's home. Her mother told me to stop pestering. They had everything under control. The others had no luck, either.

❧❧

Summer is supposed to be lovely, but things seemed pretty bleak. Bad news and bad weather. That summer measured the hottest on record with the lowest amounts of precipitation in recorded history. You could call it being baked in an oven of our own design. Off the coast of Texas colossal storms gathered momentum, sucking the ocean dry to dump onto either the Eastern seaboard of the U.S. or the Caribbean and Mexico. No one knew which way the witches' brew would be spilled; all people could do was try to prepare, but prepare for what? The unpredictable future of climate change was again up for debate on every channel, in every magazine and newspaper. The volatility of the planet was only matched by the volatility of the debate as the storms continued to threaten havoc. The sun remained in hibernation, yet at night clouds made way for the moon. Its light shone brightly, clear as day against the black backdrop of space, giving us a false sense of calm.

I suppose it was calm up there because all the humans are down here. Was this hell? Global bad news, political bad news—we were used to hearing about the chaos at the border, but young women were going missing locally. Cops called them runaways or high-risk youth, but their families disagreed. They spoke out anonymously because they feared their status in the country. Some did not have American citizenship and others were the children of immigrants. They wouldn't be kicked out before they knew the whereabouts of their missing.

Two days later Mrs. Garcia showed up at Sonic at the end of my shift looking like a bull that lost the fight. She scanned the fast food menu in disgust, and then looked at me with the same revulsion. My hair and skin were a pile of oil and sweat as the air-conditioning only worked at half capacity, the small space all counter and kitchen. The overworked machinery couldn't handle extra bodies in here. All I had were syrupy lime slushies to keep me cool with the heat of the kitchen at my back and the heat from the outside blasting my face whenever the doors were opened.

"May I take your order, Mrs. Garcia? Fernanda always orders the chili dog and tater tots."

"How will you ever learn to cook eating junk like this? Don't expect to keep that figure, either. One baby and that will be it for you."

More anger I almost couldn't temper. She didn't know that I had to prepare meals most nights for my entire family. My sisters needed to eat, and the adults had to work. I was fucking good at cooking, too.

Our eyes locked in a battle both of us would lose no matter who fired first. Mrs. Garcia leaned in toward me.

"I think my daughter needs a priest, an exorcism. Her behavior is unnatural."

Her voice became a frantic whisper.

"She is doing sexual things to herself and just yesterday she bit my hand when I tried to wipe her face. She has always been a clean girl, but her room is a mess. I need you to tell a priest exactly what you did. What spell did you use, bruja?" Her tone turned to acid. "You probably want to keep her here because you aren't good enough to make it anywhere else. I'm surprised you aren't pregnant by now."

I hated this woman. The only thing you hear where I come from is *don't get pregnant*. Don't get pregnant because that is always the beginning for us, a prophecy of failure come true. All the pointed fingers could say, "See! Not just stereotypes. Another one is born!"

We were modern girls. We knew where Planned Parenthood was, at least the ones that remained open. It made me almost wish I had been born without a womb so that no man would want me and no God would expect me to be leashed. The rest of me could be mine, and mine alone.

Mrs. Garcia wanted to see me cry, to cast her own guilt spell on me. How much she loved Fernanda was borderline obsessive, a red cape before her eyes. But I understood. When you aren't white or don't come from a place of privilege, the world needs a compelling, tangible reason to say you belong. Otherwise, you're just like the rest.

Speak, I told myself. I would use this unexpected visit to my advantage.

"Let us see her first."

She glared at me in silence, still waiting to hear me beg. I kept my best Alamo face on, hard and strong.

"Fine. Tomorrow at ten in the morning. But only you. I don't want a bunch of people in my house to whisper and spread gossip about my Fernanda. If you are late, forget about it."

I knew this was a huge win even if the others were not welcome. They knew Mrs. Garcia and would understand. We could meet after.

Our conversation had eaten up the remainder of my shift and it was time to finally leave. I could have asked her for a ride home, but my pride would not allow it. The rest of the team was scheduled until closing and I didn't want to wait. I would walk home that night because there wasn't enough money for gas until payday.

The journey from Sonic to my home was along Military Highway, a long stretch of two-way traffic with no sidewalk, only grass and trees, the street lights few and far between. When cars slowed down, my heart sped up as I readied my body to run into the woods and hide. There is no sound along that stretch of road except the whooshing of cars or the music escaping open windows. As I walked along with a key wedged between my knuckles, a slight breeze blew against the trees and my overheated skin. I told myself only deer and raccoons dwelled in the darkness as I continued to take big steps through the ankle-length dry grass.

"Hey, need a ride?"

I turned to a Volkswagen that had pulled up beside me. A couple the same age as my parents—and just as nondescript—gave me a smile. There was a collection of pine tree-shaped deodorizers hanging from their rearview mirror in a long tail. The windows in the back seat were smudged and dirty with handprints, like my parent's car but without car seats.

The man spoke this time, leaning over the woman. A Dallas Cowboys baseball cap shaded the top half of his face. "It's dangerous to be walking home this late on a road like this. Cars go real fast here. Your family must worry. You live close?"

"I don't need a ride. Thanks . . . seeing my boyfriend."

"Well, you be safe now." The woman rolled up her window, and they pulled away. When their taillights were mere red eyes in the distance, I sprinted as hard as I could through overgrown dry grass and weeds. Thank God it was a full moon; otherwise, I would not have found my way home as quickly as I did.

I cried after closing my bedroom door, feeling trapped in the dark. Eventually I composed myself, and after a few sniffs and a wipe of my eyes I called Ana.

"Hey. You still awake?"

Ana moaned on the other end of the phone. "I am now. What's up? Any news about Fernanda?"

"Yeah, I am seeing her tomorrow. I was thinking we could all meet after. You around?"

Ana yawned. "Text me what time and I'll meet you there with the others if they can make it."

"It will have to wait. Mrs. Garcia said only one."

"Pfft. I am not surprised. Well, let us know."

There was a pause. "Hey, you all right?" she asked softly.

I waited to answer. It was too late to burden anyone. "You know me. I'm always all right."

"See you tomorrow, then."

I hung up not knowing if I was all right or not. I could hear the raised voices of my mother and stepfather. It didn't matter what they fought over; this scenario was a constant when he was at home. His extended periods away made day-to-day life difficult for my mother in caring for a family, but she seemed more at ease with herself when he was gone. That relationship crumbled day by day. It was only a matter of time before it would fall apart.

I lay back down and put my pillow over my head to cover my ears because it was too late to play music. I felt broken inside.

Chapter 3

"It looks like a training bra! What is this abuelita shit?" The three girls giggled as they tossed her bra around the locker room like a volleyball. "I know . . . we should take it to the quad. Let everyone see."

Fernanda looked on helplessly, her cheeks and neck hot as she tried to cover her bare breasts. She didn't know if she should try to fight back or call for help. Both would leave her even more exposed. She'd have to let her breasts be on show, or be called a snitch for the rest of high school. Nobody lives that label down.

"Please stop." Her voice cracked, not much higher than a whisper from trying to hold back tears.

Gloria, Vanessa, and Mercedes had done this before, back in sixth grade. They'd followed her in a circle shouting insults because she consistently made the best grades and the teacher proudly announced it in front of the class. Fernanda the example. They never touched her, but a fist would have hurt less than their taunts. She didn't tell her mother to avoid being labelled a snitch. She just kept to herself even more.

Pauline walked out of the showers with the towel around her waist. "The fuck is going on here?"

"Just a little fun. Your homegirl needs a lesson. She thinks she is better than us. She ain't."

"Give me her bra back, now. What's so funny about it, anyway? I know you get your panties at Walmart like the rest of us. Get the fuck out and leave her alone before I come over there and fuck you up. I'm not even playin' now."

Gloria sucked her teeth and rolled her eyes. "You her watch dog now? Eating her pussy after school? Cuz I know she never had a man. You certainly look like a dog."

Pauline lunged towards Gloria, her towel threatening to fall to the floor.

The three girls backed away laughing. "Hey, Fernanda, you know Pauline is only your friend because you can help her with her work. Nobody likes you . . . boring bitch."

They left in a fit of laughter to another row of lockers, tossing the plain white, wireless full cup bra with thick straps into a puddle of water. Fernanda reached down and grabbed the sodden fabric.

"Dumb cabronas. They'll all be pregnant by twenty. You all right, Fernanda?"

Fernanda turned to face her locker, trembling, squeezing her eyes shut. She wanted to stuff her bra into her mouth to prevent herself from sobbing. The vulgarity of the insults. The hatred. She didn't understand why it was directed at her. Be smart, but not too smart. Be beautiful, but not so pretty as to make other females mad. Be successful, but not bossy or overly ambitious. Nobody likes a mouthy brown woman. Be a declawed kitten.

"You know none of what they said is true . . . "

Fernanda opened her eyes. "I know. You make those good grades on your own. But I am boring."

"Seriously, though. Guys don't care what kinda bra you wear, as long as they get to see titties and ass. Dogs. I had a guy try to take my tampon out while we made out. Dirty dogs."

Fernanda blushed and tried to chuckle over the sensation of wanting to vomit. She couldn't imagine even allowing anyone near *there* at that time of the month.

"I'm so embarrassed. And then saying you eat my . . . in front of everyone. My mom buys my bras and underwear with me. She says white cotton is best because it breathes, and nobody should be looking at what I wear underneath, anyway.

"I mean your mom isn't entirely wrong. Cotton is pretty damn comfortable and easy to wash, but if you want someone to look, there's nothing wrong with that. You're beautiful."

Fernanda could feel herself shrinking at this conversation. Pauline's thumb brushed her bare back as she pulled Fernanda's hair from her face. Her touch felt soft and comforting on her flesh, usually hidden behind fabric. Someone telling her she was beautiful. It made her especially uncomfortable because Pauline stood there half naked, acting like she was fully clothed in the cafeteria. Fernanda didn't want to go through high school feeling so naked and scared.

◇◇

The next morning when I went to see Fernanda, her aunt, Yolanda, answered the door in her blue scrubs. She was a pediatric nurse and always at the house. I assumed she was there to check on Fernanda's health because she answered with a blood pressure cuff in her hand and a look of worry on her face. Father Moreno sipped coffee in the living room as he listened to a tearful Mrs. Garcia.

"I caught her with that black makeup and touching herself! I left for a moment to make food before I heard moaning. Disgraceful. Disgusting. This isn't right, Father." Mrs. Garcia's voice warbled in dramatic hysterics; I could swear she was the one possessed. "My daughter is a good girl, a smart girl. She is going to college on a scholarship. We have worked hard to save for those years. Save her, Father Moreno!"

I hated how she thought of us as little girls. Maybe Mrs. Garcia would want to hear about the time I met a man five years older than myself at a poetry reading at Barnes & Noble. When the event was over, he invited me for a coffee in the café; I told him to take me back to his home. Behind his expression of hesitation and disbelief, I could sense his excitement about an aggressive nineteen-year-old. I fucked him, not because of anything he said or did, but because I wanted to. It was the first time I experienced oral sex while "Bette Davis Eyes" by Kim Carnes played on his stereo. His uncertainty turned me on as he kept asking me if it was okay. Did I like that? What did I like? I didn't have answers. That was why I was there. I didn't want to bother saving myself for anyone special because my body didn't need saving.

His bed smelled of unwashed skin and detergent, but not unpleasant. Experienced taste buds brushed unexplored nerve endings between my legs, digging a hole to my reservoir of desire. A filthy place licked clean. In that moment I felt invincible and hungry, like a vampire. I couldn't believe how mesmerized he seemed by a body I felt was too short, brown, and round to be beautiful enough to wield this kind of power. As he orgasmed, I could have done anything to him, including slashing his throat. He lay so helpless pinned beneath my grinding hips as his body went rigid and his hands gripped my thighs like a life raft that would prevent him from drowning. It felt empowering to leave when I wanted, knowing I would never return. He tried to give me his phone number and email address, but I wasn't interested. I had seen how that story plays out. I didn't know how to orgasm with a man back then, but the excitement that ran through my blood that night still makes my body shiver.

The priest, Father Moreno, cross-examined me for half an hour with Bible in hand. He looked worn, as worn as his Bible. Gold lettering that spelled his name and *The Holy Bible* was a faded print that looked like it had been rubbed too many times. Did he think God would answer him like a genie? If only that was true. Before my eighteenth birthday I attended church twice a week, and not once did a descending dove or the jabbering of tongues occur. My skeptical thoughts remained as silent as the God I sometimes tried to plead and bargain with. By the intensity emanating from the priest's eyes, this was much worse than some silly game of truth or dare. He sat next to me, placing his hand over mine.

"Lourdes. You are not in trouble. But I need to know a few things. Did you recite incantations you might have found on the internet or library, or that you made up? Are you interested in black magic?"

I wanted to laugh. I knew I wasn't in trouble. I couldn't help it if they thought of me as trouble. And was he for real? Incantations? I gave him a feeble shake of my head, avoiding eye contact so he wouldn't see me mocking him in my mind.

"Did you promise your soul to evil for money or power? A better life? Even if any of this was in jest."

He was for real and taking this seriously. Those questions were rich coming from someone who had never even met me before. The entire conversation sounded like it came from a bad horror film.

"Did you do *filthy* things to each other?"

Now he was just another pervert in disguise, like this waiter at Shoney's who gave me a slice of free pie when I was ten years old. I told my mother I didn't want it. The waiter frightened me as he stood too close whenever at our table, but she said I was being rude and to never reject things offered for free. We don't get the luxury of free things very often. Smile and be grateful. He watched behind the counter as I ate every bite. His stare sucked me in whenever I opened my mouth. To this day, that waiter makes me shiver in revulsion.

Under any other circumstances I would have told the priest to go fuck himself, literally. He would feel better after. But I knew it would make things worse for Fernanda.

"Never."

Yolanda and Mrs. Garcia yelped and cried after each question, keeping a close eye on my answers, searching for solid proof of me being no good. The priest remained stoic, but relished every second. I played dumb for twenty minutes, and then he left us to see Fernanda. Feigning ignorance is the only way to placate some people.

The two women sat at the table talking quietly so I couldn't overhear their conversation. The way Yolanda kept darting her eyes in my direction gave me the feeling they were scheming about how to ask me to leave.

Before either did, Father Moreno rushed out with bloodshot eyes. His lips were a bluish hue, as if starved of oxygen. He sputtered and emitted a choking sound as he gulped air, the kind of retching you do when liquid spills down the wrong pipe. Tears and saliva covered his ashen face. He pressed the Bible across his heart. With a voice too shaken to have any authority, he cried, "Lock that girl up in an institution. Nothing can save her! She is ruined."

Mrs. Garcia resumed her wailing as he slammed the front door behind him.

I didn't know what could have possibly happened in that room, but I had to speak. All the times I had felt silenced had formed a voice in my head, a voice that wouldn't leave me until it could be heard.

"Let me see her now. You can't exorcise her. She isn't possessed. And she is not a lost cause. Let me find a way. Fuck that priest and fuck anyone that tells us we are crazy!" I screamed this with the same fervor I'd had the night of the séance, calling for a spirit.

Before Mrs. Garcia or Yolanda could respond, music began playing so loud the bass vibrated against the door. The three of us reared our heads towards Fernanda's bedroom. Since she wasn't allowed to go to concerts or to the annual Fiesta in downtown San Antonio, her dad had spared no expense on the stereo she'd received two Christmases before.

Mrs. Garcia sneered at me in contempt. "What do you know, stupid girl? I'll keep with my faith and my way."

She didn't tell me to leave, giving me an opportunity as small as a crescent moon, but I held fast to it. Until I came up with a plan, I would help to care for my friend.

"I'm going in there."

Mrs. Garcia and Yolanda continued to glare at me hard, wishing my existence away, but didn't try to stop me. Maybe they were even a little scared of me from my outburst.

Part of me feared what I would see in that bedroom. Would she be using a cross like a dildo like in the Director's Cut version of The Exorcist? Did she try to seduce the priest? As far as I knew, Fernanda was still a virgin.

I opened the door to her room, determined not to be afraid. "Rhythm Is Gonna Get You" by Gloria Estefan and the Miami Sound Machine crashed and flooded around me. Her room was nicely decorated, unlike mine, which I painted to have the color and texture of cold stone, like a crypt. It wasn't my intention at the time, but I thought it would look nice with the red curtains that matched my favorite pillowcases and sheets. Fernanda's room was covered in white lace, with dolls she kept from her childhood, family photos, little gifts given to her for communion and birthdays. Like a museum to her life, and nearly spotless except for the debris from her hair and mud smudged on her windowsill.

Fernanda sat at her armoire untangling her dirty hair and singing to herself. The black makeup looked greasy on her unwashed skin. She looked up at me with a grin as wide as that first night.

"Here, let me help," I offered as I moved to her side. Her pupils quivered; was it Fernanda or the inhabitant from the séance? I smiled and danced in place while smoothing out hair I hoped she would agree to wash.

"What did you tell the priest? He ran out fast," I said, jokingly.

Her giggle sounded closer to a growl.

"I asked him if he wanted to eat my sin." She opened her legs so I could see in the mirror she wasn't wearing any underwear. "That man has just as much sin inside of him as everyone else. *She* told me. Who is he to tell me I'm evil? Who anointed him?"

I couldn't argue with her. "He looked terrible when he came out. What did you do?"

She continued to tug on the frayed balls of tangled hair. "I don't know. I didn't do anything. She did. I can't remember. As soon as I touched him, it was like being pulled under by big waves. The kind that leave you afraid, but excited. Saltwater in your nose, stinging your eyes as you roll around underwater. It happens so fast you don't realize what's happening. And then you come up for air. Anyway, he made it out of here alive. What's the problem? Maybe he will be less of a jackass now."

The boldness of my friend shocked me. I was the ill-tempered, foul-mouthed one. Fernanda was the brainy girl with a shy smile. In the back of my mind, I always felt concerned that Fernanda ran the risk of being taken advantage of or intimidated once she left for school. I worried she would meet a guy not as smart as her but who would want to own her, make her feel she wasn't as capable as everyone knew she was. Or she would have a boss who would convince her the only way was the horizontal way because that's how business is done.

Her hair was still a rat's nest of dirt after what seemed like an eternity picking through it. It would take

some time to untangle. As I started again at the crown of
her head, she stopped me with her hand on mine. "Did
you like it?"

"What do you mean?"

"Sex? Did you like it?"

"It was good. I think. I want more practice. You
want to cleanse me of my sin?" I chuckled and danced in
place to the beat of the music.

She turned back to the mirror to let me continue
with her hair.

"No, silly. She says you don't have the kind of sin she
eats. But I want to go to Planeta tonight."

I stopped plucking at her hair, trying to make eye
contact through the mirror. Fernanda never wanted
to go to Planeta. Correction: she was never allowed.
Planeta is a small club off the River Walk that played the
hottest Latin, freestyle, and hip-hop. They also served
minors. The few times I went, I blew off as much steam
as I could because I knew it might mean I would have to
sleep on the side porch. If I came home past curfew, the
chains on the inside of all the doors would be fastened in
place. No one would wake up in the middle of the night
to let me in. Texas summer nights remained warm, so it
wasn't that bad lying on a metal bench falling asleep to
the stars. If someone snatched me in the night, it would
be as if someone came to collect the trash.

"Fernanda, we can go, but you need to tell me who *she* is."

Her pupils quivered, although they were still her own. "I don't know, Lourdes. Honest. I don't know. She isn't bad to me or unkind, I promise, and she would never hurt you or the girls. I know that. She tried to tell me her name, but I couldn't understand it. When she speaks in my head, I can hear her the way we speak now. Other times I go blank; the other language is too much for me. It's like her language is in a different frequency."

I knew she was telling me the truth, or at least believed what she was saying.

"What about *you*, Fernanda? I don't want her to hurt you." I bent forward towards the mirror with both hands flat against the top and met her gaze.

A flicker of light from her pupils made me draw back. Was it possible the two personalities were existing simultaneously? I held my fear close to me, like the priest with his Bible. There was nothing I could do in this situation but observe and take mental notes. Something had stirred inside of her, and I didn't want to anger the entity, despite Fernanda saying it would not harm either of us.

"Okay. We can go tonight but you need to wash yourself."

"Maybe Ruben can take us?"

"Why?"

She blushed. I had seen that blossom of crimson on her cheeks before when it came to Ruben. "Because we want to drink. Someone has to drive."

A good point. I'd text Pauline and the rest of the girls to let them know about the evening's festivities. Before she left to shower, I asked a question.

"You got a thing for Ruben? It's okay. He's pretty cute."

"Maybe. Go home and get ready." She flashed me a flirtatious smile. My friend was changing—for good or bad, I didn't know yet.

When Mrs. Garcia saw Fernanda acting as if nothing was wrong, the anger flared up again. "Bruja, if I find out you have bewitched her . . . "

I matched her aggressive stance. The new voice would not be tamed for anyone or anything. It felt good. "Mrs. Garcia, I haven't done anything. You really think if I had that power I would still be living at home or working at Sonic? Back off my ass."

She had nothing to say. With a huff she walked past me, carrying a folded stack of Fernanda's fresh clothes.

I left feeling excited about the night ahead. What could go wrong when girls want to have fun?

❧❧

Father Moreno squeezed and rubbed the flaccid rosary in his hand, allowing the sharp edges of the metal crucifix to dig into his skin. It was a pain that he felt he deserved for allowing his faith to be tainted by desire. Though there was no confession at this time, he liked to sit in the small square booth that resembled a closet, a safe quiet place. His mind and body needed sequestering to make sense of what had occurred at the Garcia house.

He'd spoken with Fernanda's friend Lourdes who he could tell was the promiscuous type, just looking for trouble in her dirty Keds, tight denim shorts, tank top that didn't cover her bra straps, and purple lipstick too dark for one so young. It didn't matter how hot the weather might be; the amount of skin on show was inappropriate. Her womanly curves were displayed in such a way that you didn't have to imagine what she would look like in the nude.

Mrs. Garcia had already warned him she was an uncooperative girl coming from a broken home and not a high achiever in school. She seemed similar to so many young women who aimlessly lived their lives through low-paying jobs and convenient relationships that never lasted, like his cousin Martha on her third child with two different fathers. If only she had given her life to God. His face still burned when he thought how he would have wanted her body and hand in marriage if they were not second cousins. There were never any other women for him. He'd hated her for ruining him like that, for coming to him to cry over men who used her or female friends that betrayed her. All he could do was listen in physical and mental frustration while offering her tissues to wipe off the mascara that blackened her face. How many times had he told her she didn't need makeup? A smile and kind heart were all she needed to be beautiful in the eyes of God, and to him. Heat traveled to the lower parts of his body as shame scalded his cheeks.

When Mrs. Garcia first told him about the situation, he hadn't believed these girls meant to conjure a demon, but their vulnerability made it easy; they were the perfect vessels of temptation, just like Martha had been. He had approached Fernanda's bedroom door feeling confident he could handle the young woman, who might just be disturbed. Mental illnesses can go undetected just like demons. Maybe she needed a doctor and medication instead of a priest. That was until he entered the room.

The young woman sat before her armoire picking muck from her scalp. As he walked closer, she shifted her eyes to him in the reflection of the mirror. They were not eyes belonging to a human. She had the eyes of a prehistoric creature, those of a caiman. Glassy green and black marbled orbs with an inky vertical slit in the middle fixed upon his face. The black lipstick and heavy eyeliner only accentuated the grotesque thing that sat before him. It could barely be called female. This was beyond any doubt a spiritual matter.

"I would like us to pray together. Your mother is very worried."

"Why is she worried? I have done nothing wrong. Maybe I should be worried about all of you making a scene."

His brain tried to reconcile her appearance with the voice of the girl. This is what he trained for. To fight the evil we are all born with.

"Our Father, who art in Heaven," he began.

Double eyelids blinked coquettishly at him as he spoke. "Stop, please. That isn't going to get you anywhere. This isn't a demonic possession. There is no devil in the biblical sense. But there is God. There are gods. We are not alone in the dark."

Her blasphemy was as distasteful as the scent of sweat on her skin. With Godly authority and confidence, he stepped closer, "The father of lies and flies would say that. Kiss this cross."

Animal eyes rolled. "Ugh. If it will make *you* feel better. We all have to make small sacrifices."

Fernanda stood before him to take the cross from his hand. As their hands touched, she gripped the crucifix tighter, pulling him to her body and scent. Lips parted enough that he could see her wet tongue running along the edges of her teeth. Vertical pupils dilated and sparked before she hissed.

"Your sin is great. Have you confessed?"

Arousal, humiliation, and revulsion stirred beneath his clothing, which felt tight around his neck and between his legs.

With strength beyond a young woman her size, she seized the back of his neck. Unable to stop himself, he opened his mouth, feeling the pit of his stomach being folded and sucked out. The secret sores festering at the bottom of his heart popped, releasing into the vapor of his breath and drifted into the girl until she reached the last, deepest sore. He focused all his hate and fear on stopping what was happening, shoving Fernanda with enough force to catapult her backwards onto her bed. Her skirt lifted to show her bare sex, a dark vertical slit like her eyes that wanted to devour him.

He could not force himself to look away until she spoke. "You can eat my sin if you like. I see what's in your heart." Before her fingertips managed to reach between her legs, he ran.

Never had temptation presented itself in such a vulgar, alluring way. Only once had he defiled his mind with pornography, when he was much younger. He still had dreams about it, and now this bruja demon had tarnished his mind in the worst way. Her wickedness would stick to him. What if this was only the beginning and this demon decided to take more innocent lives? Something drastic had to be done.

Chapter 4

We met at the end of Fernanda's road at 10 p.m. Ruben was waiting in his black Chevy truck, Pauline at his side. We climbed into the back seat. It smelled like shoe shine and his cologne.

"Hey, Lourdes."

"Hi, Ruben. Thanks for the ride so late. Hope you didn't have plans tonight."

"Well, Pauline said you were going out and no way was she going to wait for a ride with all the weird shit happening. It's dangerous. And no plans." He glanced at us in the rearview mirror.

"My big brother. The Mexican Knight Rider in his truck that I will get when he moves." Pauline slapped her hands together and grinned, scanning the car.

"You doing okay, Fernanda? You look nice."

Fernanda smiled and nodded to Pauline.

"You ladies call about half an hour before you want to go. I don't want you waiting on any corners. Deal?"

Pauline and I mumbled, "Yeah."

The inhabitant remained quiet the entire journey; however, Fernanda's pupils vibrated, the color changing as we sat in the back of the truck. Ruben kept glancing back at Fernanda and me in the mirror, but I don't think he noticed with the passing shadows of streetlights and underpasses, and the dark makeup ringing her eyes.

The club was packed as usual. Red and blue strobe lights made the dance floor look like hell's waiting room. Bass beat against our chests, war drums to signal a good time ahead. I wore my good top, the velour one the color of ox blood with spaghetti straps, paired with jeans. Lipstick the same shade as my top, because the darker the better. It made me look badass. Fernanda's hair fell to the center of her back in a French braid. She wore a cropped white halter top without a bra. Mrs. Garcia would never allow her to wear that out with the way it clung to her chest. Baggy jeans cinched at the waist like mine. Her lips were still lined and slathered in black, as were her eyes, except it was no longer messy.

The original bruja *Craft* crew met by a speaker. Perla sat on one of the speakers wiggling to Lisa Lisa and Cult Jam with drink in hand, her neck craning over the crowd in anticipation of our arrival. I'd texted them that there would be a reunion here tonight because I didn't want to babysit alone, plus maybe this is what we all needed, to be together and unafraid. Our combined friendship could be powerful medicine for our friend.

"What are you sad bitches up to?"

Perla hopped off the speaker to give Fernanda a hug.

"We fucking missed you! I'm sorry we haven't been around. We've been scared and your mom didn't want anyone around. Lourdes said she had a handle on things." Fernanda shrugged her shoulders and took the drink from Perla, chugging it down like it was Kool-Aid.

"¡Orale!" Ana shouted. Everyone was happy to have their homegirl back.

Everything seemed calm at the club, Fernanda's eyes back to normal. In that moment, it felt okay to relax and get a drink from the bar as we were with our friends. If there was a night to take off scrimping and saving, it was tonight. Bars are always shitty waiting places with someone trying to cut in or spilling alcohol on your clothes or hair, and it always takes longer than you think. Whenever I glanced back, dancing bodies prevented me from seeing our group. This made me nervous but not nervous enough to leave the line. When I returned to the speaker the girls were talking among themselves, obviously tipsy, but Fernanda was gone.

I'd fucked up again. I'd be damned if she lost her virginity or got assaulted by some guy in a grimy bathroom stall.

"Where is Fernanda? Everyone needs to find Fernanda. I'll check the bathrooms, you three spread out, find her, now!"

Ana looked around. "She was just here. Quiet, but here. How did she get away without us noticing?"

"Is she not okay?" Perla had that same look of fear as the first night. She could sense the panic in my voice. I had to cool it.

"She is getting better. Just want to be sure. Don't worry or panic. It will make things worse."

Perla obeyed, leaving her drink on the speaker to make her way through the crowd. It was difficult to see with so little light. Multicolored lasers slashed erratically at the dark, making faces unrecognizable; bass and electronic beats came from all directions, disorienting me. The music made me feel dizzy. *Move,* I told myself. *Bathrooms.* I shoved through bodies, trying to appear drunk. I felt sorry for being rude, but I didn't need beef from anyone. Everyone makes way for the petite inebriated chick who can't hold her liquor and needs the bathroom before she pukes on their shoes. Every female and male looked identical grinding or jumping to the music. It was so easy to get lost or lose sight of someone. The sensory overload made me want to vomit.

There she was. The bitterness of the oversweetened cranberry juice mixed with cheap vodka stabbed within my stomach, sloshing violently as a guy led her into the men's bathroom. My mouth tasted like nail polish remover. I tried to rush as quickly as possible through the crowd, my adrenaline spiking, afraid of what he would try and how she would handle it. Like Fernanda or the inhabitant with the priest?

I burst through the door. A single dude zipped up his fly. He looked at me, and then at the last stall with a quick flick of his head. The smell of piss and pot filled the air like burning incense, stinging my nostrils. I opened the stall ready to raise hell only to see that Fernanda wasn't Fernanda. Her body was pressed against some guy, charcoal fingertips wrapped around his throat. Tendrils of black and red radiated from where his skin touched hers. Fernanda's black lipstick was smeared on his face, which was turning from purple to blue. But it was her tongue that made me shiver in the claustrophobic, sweltering bathroom. It appeared bright crimson with raised bumps pumping and prodding his like one snake devouring another. Strands of saliva dribbled out of both of their mouths. Her throat bulged and contracted with unnatural elasticity like she was swallowing something. Pupils lit by candle flames swung in my direction. She let go of the paralyzed man. Chest heaving, a low, husky moan escaped her mouth with every slow breath.

I tried to steady my horror, looking directly into her inhuman, double-lidded eyes. The vertical black slits were surrounded by shades of green and yellow like a brackish pool of water.

"Fernanda. Please speak to me. Come back."

The thing ran her tongue across her lips and cocked her chin, nostrils flaring like an animal sensing something approaching. Fernanda's face went slack as her body convulsed violently. One of her hands had crushed a water bottle that was on the verge of splitting in two. I rushed at her, afraid she would collapse against the toilet. I needed help but knew the others wouldn't understand. I was on my own. I took the bottle of water, hoping a drink might aid her recovery. As I opened the cap and brought it to her mouth, she shrieked, "No!" and knocked it onto the unconscious or dead guy slumped against the sharpie-graffitied wall.

Fernanda was back, her pleading eyes filled with tears. Her pupils fluctuated, trying to find their original shape.

"He drugs women. He is so bad. Check his pockets if you don't believe me. It was so ugly what I saw him do. But we ate his sin."

There were voices in the bathroom. Trying not to make a sound, I locked the door and then leaned down to assess his condition. His pulse was weak but he was alive as far as I could tell. If he was in fact trying to drug females, he could be in Satan's bed for all I cared. More justice in this toilet than out in the world. I kneeled on the yellowed dirty floor to search his pockets and found keys, cash, credit cards, ID, and a bag of pills.

"Take it." Fernanda spoke with an authority that she'd never asserted before, but this time in her own voice. She looked at the body with curiosity. The sadness of moments ago was now a cold hardness. Silent rage. I knew it. I carried it like a purse.

I looked up at Fernanda for any sign the inhabitant might return. "I don't want those pills," I said. "Call the police; there is money and pills. I'm sure he will get charged for something."

"No. Keep the money. You need it. For school. Looks like a few hundred."

"Thou shalt not steal." I was a poor man's Mrs. Garcia. As much as I wanted the money, I didn't want to get into trouble.

"Eye for an eye," she retorted.

"Vengeance is *mine,* sayeth the Lord." I wasn't afraid of the inhabitant. Time served in church had left me prepared for holy war.

Fernanda softened and kneeled next to me. "Lourdes, you will never get ahead if you don't take every opportunity. Come on, you're smarter than this. We will be blamed. Not him. We are underage, drinking, wearing makeup, looking for trouble. Look at that top you're wearing with your chichis looking all perky."

For once, I was good cop and she was bad. I couldn't argue. Fuck it. I flushed the pills down the toilet and took the cash. The boys on Wall Street get bonuses, some stole millions. Hell, there were governments that siphoned off entire countries. Could the inhabitant swallow all their sin? Plus the money would come in handy because I had a feeling my mother might need to borrow it.

The voices had left by this time. I unlocked the door and peered out to be sure. Nothing. We cleaned Fernanda's face with a rough paper towel, then walked out to everyone in the club. Ana, Perla, and Pauline were huddled at the bar looking like they were trying to hatch a plan for the worst possible outcome they could think of.

"What you pendejas clucking about?"

"¡Dios! Jesus! Fernanda, you scared us! What happened?" Ana threw her arms around us.

"She was talking to some dude. I got to talking to his friend. Let's get out of this place. You go first. I need to pee."

I nodded my head to Fernanda with a knowing look before walking to the least populated part of the bar to flag one of the male bartenders.

"Hey, there is a dude in the toilet that isn't doing so well. You need to get him some help. Think it's drugs." Before he could stop me or ask questions, I feigned loud tipsiness to get out the door and into the freshness of the night.

The girls laughed outside while Ana lit a fresh joint. I watched Fernanda, terrified and curious. What was happening to my friend? I mentally beat myself up thinking back on that night of the séance. What if everyone was right and I am just a bad piece of flesh? What if I'm the problem that caused this to happen?

I thought I was accustomed to the feeling of running out of options, but this felt like being buried alive.

🐛🐛

Fernanda lay in bed, buzzing from the experience at the club.

"That was amazing . . . what we did to that asshole. I can't wait to do it again. I wish I could be like that all the time."

My dear, power is as delicate as the skin of a grape, intoxicating when it ferments and grows and like an unattended vine if not pruned. Where I am from, our power increases over centuries and millennia. Knowing oneself takes time. Harnessing that power even longer.

Fernanda licked her lips, left dry by the matte lipstick. "I'm sorry—I know it's bad for me to take joy from knocking his ass out. I often feel excited and then ashamed. If I think about my accomplishments too much I'm a show-off. If I think about sex I'm a slut."

Labels by others are a way to control you. Hear it enough and you will believe it, like a spell.

Fernanda thought of Adam and Eve, the forbidden fruit of the apple. How knowledge made Eve into something to be renounced.

"I don't want to be afraid of my body anymore. I want to know more about it, what it craves."

Remember what I said about power. Delicate touch.

Fernanda unbuttoned her jeans and slipped her hand over her panties.

Fernanda, you do not need that thin barrier. Feel and see your body.

Fernanda took a breath and pulled off her jeans and panties.

A heaviness settled into the front of Fernanda's brain, the voice in her head a soft melody. *Relax. Relax your mind and open yourself wide enough to let something enter or exit, even if it's just yourself.*

Fernanda thought of the first time she kissed Ruben, after the barbeque. For a year before that she'd burned in secret for him; they'd exchanged long glances even when he had a girlfriend. The opportunity arose when Pauline slept at Ana's one night, passed out from mixing weed and beer. It was just the two of them when he drove her home. So close, but still hesitant. When he parked his truck, neither said goodbye.

"Maybe I can call you sometime?" Ruben's clear skin and long eyelashes made Fernanda want to be closer. A light wetness on his lips felt like an invitation.

"I would like that." She didn't know what she was waiting for until he leaned over to turn down the radio. With a thundering pulse, she turned her head towards his, allowing gravity to bring them together. His soft tongue slipped between her lips. It felt like magic between her legs, sparks of energy. In her shyness and fear of what could happen next, she had pulled away and said goodbye.

Fernanda didn't want to hesitate any longer. Splayed out on her bed with a mirror propped between her legs as instructed by the goddess, she thought of how his body looked beneath his cadet uniform. Those full lips that were pillowed and tender. Perla's sexual adventures always stirred something inside of her. Now Fernanda felt the goddess ease the guilt ingrained since before her first communion, the white veil hanging on her wall a constant reminder.

If our bodies are something to be ashamed of, why are they created so? If pleasure was not to be ours, why are we built to feel it?

The folds between her legs looked like purple and pink petals shimmering with morning dew the more aroused she became. Her index finger stroked her flesh sending a feeling of calm through her, a warmth that extended to her thighs and nipples, like the only time she took a drag of weed from a small glass pipe, but without the hacking cough after. What if it wasn't her finger but Ruben's, or even better those lips of his, pressing gently and then harder. Fernanda leaned back in her bed, forgetting the mirror. Why did she deny herself this for so long?

Fernanda continued her exploration. The longer she became acquainted with herself, the less shame she felt. It dissolved like a host on the tongue.

Fernanda, I still have work to do through you. Tomorrow I will concentrate my power to break through our physical and mental barriers. I will move into the light which means you will be suspended in darkness with no recollection or control.

"Absolutely. You can have all of me."

Power surged within Fernanda. First busting that pig at the club and now saying what she felt. Even if the voice wasn't a goddess but a devil, it was worth it. This freedom.

Chapter 5

After the club things went from normal-strange to desperate-scary. I showed up at Fernanda's house in a good mood the next day, expecting the Fernanda from the previous night. Her father opened the door in his postal uniform. He appeared groggy, his eyelids thicker and heavier than before.

"I don't think it's a good idea for you to be here," he said.

"Why? What happened?" He opened the door just wide enough for me to see Fernanda sitting on the sofa and muttering to herself like a zombie.

"My wife said not to let anyone in today. I'm sorry." He shut the door.

The rest of the girls and I drove slowly past her house every day. Fernanda returned to the dying flower beds to bleed and mutter in Nahuatl in the relentless heat. The hot sunless haze felt like some spell. Under no circumstances could water be used for outdoor purposes. Pick any street and the grass in front of every house looked like a yellowed bruise. Waterparks and car washes were suspended. The reservoir was at a critical level, leaving the land bone dry.

Despite the heat, a charity scheduled a vigil on the UTSA campus for the girls who had gone missing in the area and for those who had lost their lives or were detained at the border. The vigil began at 10 p.m. so that the temperature would be bearable. The moon shone brighter than ever in a cloudless sky. I decided to go with Ana, Perla, and Pauline. Fernanda was not herself enough to attend but I would take photos and videos to show her. I hoped messages from her friends would lure her out.

A swell of people showed up including camera crews from local TV stations. It was uplifting to see that even though it was an unsociable hour, people did care. Ana bought the candles from a charity collecting money for undocumented immigrants. Standing in front of the library, we each held a thin wax stick inside a paper cup with a hole at the bottom and a green ribbon tied in a bow around the top.

"What's new with Fernanda?" asked Ana before the speeches began on the steps of the library. "My mom says people at church are talking because almost every priest has been called to that house."

"Nothing. It is all the same and I'm out of ideas. Say a prayer for her. Okay?"

Pauline gave me side-eye. "You don't believe, and you're telling us to pray? We need to do something!"

I didn't want a fight, not now, but she was right. Thankfully, the vigil was starting, giving everyone an excuse not to talk about what weighed heavily upon us. We sang songs in Spanish (except me, I only know the chorus to Selena songs) and hymns in English. Families spoke in turn about their experiences and thanked everyone for their support. I took a video of the crowd to capture this moment of unity and care for those usually relegated to soundbites.

A sense of melancholy descended upon the crowd as the vigil concluded, our hopes floating to the sky with the smoke of the burnt-out candles. As I scanned the ofrenda with my phone, a couple kneeling among the cluster of items caught my eye. The woman slipped her hand into the bed of flowers and plucked one out. She then tried to stealthily reach for a photo of a child no older than ten. The man said something and pointed at an object. The woman reached for a small panda Beanie Baby.

"Hey! Stop that! You!" She looked straight at me, startled. The man grabbed her arm and forcefully pulled her away.

"Girls come with me!" The couple weaved between people, moving too fast for me to catch up. The woman kept looking back at me until they disappeared into the crowd. I stopped abruptly.

Pauline caught up to me.

"What was that all about? What is going on with you now?" She wasn't angry so much as confused.

"Someone was trying to steal a photo and a toy from the flowers. They looked kinda familiar, but I don't know. Who would steal from a vigil? Fucking loonies."

Perla shook her head. "This shit is getting so strange it's making my head spin."

"I promise we will get through this and get Fernanda to school in the fall," I said.

"What did we do that night, Lourdes?" Pauline bowed her head trying to hold back her tears.

Perla put her arms around her. "We didn't do anything."

Pauline looked at the last of the candles burning next to the flowers and photos. "Like this? This is all one master plan of pain and hate. None of these people deserve to be just photographs. How are we supposed to keep going if there is no road, or signs, fucking nada!"

She was right. What was any of this?

I spent the night at Ana's house because I needed a bed, not the bench on the side of my house. For the first time in a long time, I was frightened by the dark. I didn't want to be alone. Seeing that woman stirred something in me, the way she looked at the photo in morbid fascination, the familiar feeling I got from her face.

Ana and I didn't speak much because we both had work early in the morning. The breakfast shift at Sonic began at 7 a.m. There also wasn't much to say because life was consumed by the possession of our friend. We kept flopping around trying to get comfortable, even though her bed was big enough for three.

"I can't sleep," Ana said.

"Me, neither. I don't know what to do. And I've been having weird dreams."

Ana turned her head towards me and propped herself up with her arm. "What of?"

"Well, one is of a woman. She looks like a caiman, stunning and powerful. The other is a little stranger, and I cannot figure it out. In my dream, I struggle to breathe. My head throbs at the temples. I'm writing notes in a battered journal overlooking the remnants of a glacier. The sun is scorching my eyes—I am either closer to it or it is closer to earth. Despite being so near to the heat, my skin aches from the cold. I feel a sense of urgency to record my thoughts."

She stared at me in the dark, and then lay on her back again.

"Let me think about it."

I took a deep breath, feeling more relaxed. If anyone could figure it out, it would be Ana.

❧❧

Words flowed from Fernanda like a chant, her inflection and speed changing too quickly for me to discern the exact words. I tried recording it to translate with Google, kneeling next to her in the dirt. It was impossible. Having just that one good night of us all together angered me. What was it all for? Why hadn't the inhabitant ventured out again since then? I decided to stop recording and switched my phone to the video of the vigil.

"Fernanda, I have a little surprise for you. The girls say hello." I placed the phone in front of her.

"Hey, baby girl. I miss you and wish you were here. We will keep you in our prayers tonight." Ana air-kissed the screen and then moved to make way for Perla.

"I'm lighting a candle for you, so you are here in spirit. Love you," she said.

Pauline was the last to speak. "We want you back, Fernanda. Whatever you need to do to come back to us." She was on the verge of tears.

Fernanda watched with a glazed look, black, full lips hanging open as she breathed through her mouth. Not a hint of emotion at seeing our little gang.

The rest of the video was of the vigil, until it came to the part with the couple at the ofrenda at the UTSA library entrance. Fernanda's legs trembled. Her head shook and eyes transformed, dilating into different shapes. Droplets of green and yellow ink leaked from her tear ducts. It was the inhabitant. She took the phone from my hand, inspecting the image until it went black. A dirt-caked fingernail tapped on the screen. She recognized them.

"What is it?" I asked. "Who are they? Do I need to find them? Tell me?!"

My raised voice must have alarmed Mrs. Garcia because she came outside. Fernanda dropped her head, shrouding her face with her hair.

"Everything okay? Do you need more water? This heat is suffocating." She looked around the yard, fanning herself with a Reader's Digest. The patio was covered with a wooden trellis that her roses had once climbed. Now, there were only woody vines without a single rosebud left.

"Aye, my poor roses. They say that this might be a sign of things to come. I can't watch the news anymore."

"We are fine. Just showing Fernanda messages from the girls."

She glanced at me and Fernanda with sad eyes before going back inside. When she left, Fernanda placed her lips to my ear. A raspy hiss, "No."

"Please speak to me, Fernanda!" I said in the loudest possible whisper.

Fernanda rapidly blinked and shook her head. "What happened?"

"Well, for starters, *she* spoke to me after I showed you a video of the vigil for the missing girls. You know I will never leave your side, but this makes no sense. To me or the girls. The club scared me, but I thought . . . I don't know. Things would be just like before . . . I don't know what I'm saying. I'm an idiot."

Fernanda's eyes widened. "What did she say? Could you understand her?"

"She didn't say anything. Made me feel like this is just craziness I don't understand."

We sat there in silence, listening to the sound of soaps coming from the TV and someone mowing their lawn nearby, until she perked up.

"Hey. You know what it's like. You know how you never let Ana make you any mixed drinks?"

I chuckled thinking of all the dumb shit we experimented with. Ana came up with some nasty concoctions. All way too strong. "Yeah, because she doesn't have the patience to measure."

"Well, the inhabitant wants to communicate with you, but the stories she wants to tell must come from her own language, her own voice and words. Not diluted.

She wants it to be strong. Straight from the bottle. And when neither of us can get through, it's like your little sisters when they were younger. Remember how mad they would get before they could talk? Their frustration knowing but not knowing how to speak. Then you would be just as fed up trying to figure out that they wanted?"

I felt less dejected after her explanation and wrapped one arm around her. "You want to see the video again?" Fernanda smiled and I pressed play.

When I lay in my bed that night, I prayed to the dark for guidance. I don't think purgatory is a place for people— it's a space for all those prayers that seem to go nowhere. Just look at the faces of the families torn apart. After a while all those hopes and wishes spread like a broken yolk over our being. Where do those spoken manifestations go? Fucking purgatory, just like an ugly Bosch painting. That's how I imagine it. So I'd fall asleep thinking of another day at Sonic taking orders in my pit-stained uniform, curse myself for being too stupid to figure this out, and then visit my friend.

◐◑

There was no change in the situation for days after showing her the video. Fernanda allowed herself to be

led to her room when she was lucid and then moved
back to the garden when the thing made an appearance.
Even in the sweltering heat, it wanted to be outside. She
would squat in the damp earth in her white cotton with
black lipstick and heavily lined eyes. You could tell when
her mother had tried to remove the makeup because the
stain of black extended beyond her lips and the edges of
her eyes. I was still adamant she didn't need a priest or
an exorcism, but there was no question that we needed
help. She couldn't go around as two people, and it was
imperative she start college in the fall. Time was running
out and after seeing what she did at the club, I feared
more for the safety of others.

The longer this carried on with no answers the more
my heart broke for my friend. I called out for something
ancient to show itself, though I didn't believe anything
would really show up. Nothing in my short goddam
life amounted to anything worthwhile. Why would
conjuring a spirit be any different?

I sat with Fernanda in the dirt and brushed her hair
while her mother wiped blood from her thighs. Any
attempt to move her before whatever was inhabiting her
was ready to move ended with a snarl and gnashing of
teeth followed by hysterical sobbing. At least she drank
and ate when offered sustenance. Fernanda's father
bought cases of Gatorade for us. I sat day after day in my

sweat, still finding it impossible to translate anything but those words from the first night: "Naqui. Niyoli." "I enter. I live."

More priests were invited by the family. They looked embarrassed at the sight of Fernanda while completely ignoring me in my bikini top and denim cutoffs. The older ones scarcely glanced in her direction, their eyes showing no compassion or real concern.

I couldn't tell if either Fernanda or the inhabitant had any awareness of these visitors. They evoked no response from her. Only when her speeches came to nothing did she react. This is when she would scrape her hands down the stems of her mother's dead roses. The petals were long gone, but the thorns remained sharp. Her palms were shredded, bloody rags she offered to me with black tears running down her face. I clasped her hands to cry with her. With her blood, she crudely wrote in the dirt, "Send them away." I tried to show Mrs. Garcia, but she dismissed it as more devil talk. "Of course a demon doesn't want priests!" she screamed in desperate frustration.

I'm surprised my body wasn't turning into a pillar of salt from all my sweat and tears. But I wasn't the only one at the end of her patience. Mrs. Garcia had begun to look for spiritual guidance elsewhere. The priests' judgments were not just reserved for Fernanda and me, but also fell upon her. What had *she* done to bring about this calamity? Yolanda suggested a curandera she knew. Maybe a cleansing from whatever was cursing them. Reluctantly, Mrs. Garcia made a list of potential enemies and prayed for forgiveness for whatever ways she might have wronged them. The home was cleansed, filling it with the scent of herbs and smoke. The curandera came and left with the same results as the priests, except one hundred dollars richer. Fernanda planted herself in the dirt, chanting louder than before to remind us the inhabitant was still there and not going anywhere until it got what it wanted, which was a mystery to us all.

Chapter 6

The smell of wood in the quiet room made it all come together. There would not be another Martha to steal his peace. No, if you build your house in Sodom and Gomorrah, expect fire and salt. Unlike the days of old, there would be actual proof. All would see the toll of worshipping Satan, and he would be exalted. All the years he'd given to Christ would finally be for something because as of late his faith had been waning in the isolating modern world.

Perhaps he would even have enough power to have a say about this new pope, so quick to give in to the liberal nature of society. Instead of enforcing the natural laws set by God, he accepted all sorts. Tears and fire, Father Moreno would have both. He prayed to God for a plan to show the world that the wages of sin is death, even if it meant this young woman would lose her life.

With that thought, he ached to speak to Martha.

He left the confessional for the back office of the church. The small space had an old brown metal desk with a wide, out-of-date desktop computer taking up most of the surface. There was also a landline phone, metal filing cabinets, and a closet for cassocks and robes. The rest of the room was filled with various statues of La Virgen that Father Moreno had been collecting ever since he was given one as a boy after having incurable night terrors. His childhood room was filled with them. In adulthood, he increased the collection. There were some as small as coins, as well as some life-sized statues. All of them unique and sacred in different ways that made him feel protected and loved.

In the corner, another door. This room was half the size of the office and used for storage. Against the wall lay a humming rectangular freezer used to store ice cream and bags of ice for social events. Father Moreno had padlocked it, the only key around his neck. He cited kids stealing the frozen treats. He unlocked the freezer and lifted the lid.

There she was, his immortalized Virgin. Her body lay in the fetal position like the sacrifices of old, arms crossed and legs drawn towards her chest. Both ankles and wrists were bound with a rosary. A lace mantilla pinned to her head glittered with ice as did the robe she wore. Ice crystals crusted her eyelashes. He brushed them away so as to see her face clearly. Her eyes were always the one thing to make him melt and wish away the cruelty of fate, that test God placed before him to prove his faith. She looked like she did when they were younger, a virgin. *His* La Virgencita always and forever.

"Hola, my dear Martha. I've missed you. You wouldn't know how lonely it can be without you. Your children are fine. Their fathers bring them to Sunday school every week. They should make you feel proud. I know it must be lonely for you, too, but not for much longer. There will be another angel joining you soon."

Eddies of cold air caressed his bare skin as he looked upon Martha with a deep yearning. Even in this state, she aroused him. He leaned over and kissed her forehead. Pangs of guilt sometimes gripped him when he saw Martha's children with their fathers, but mostly because of the thoughts of what their children would have been like, had their love not been deemed a test.

"Soon I will have a collection of angels for myself and for the glory of God."

Father Moreno closed the freezer and made sure it was securely locked, placing the key back around his neck beside a small vial of Martha's blood and tears. He'd collected them as a relic as she lay dying. Relics are powerful things. As the life drained from her body, he held the vial to his own cheeks so their fluids might mingle on this earth. He wore it always, touching it before bed as if it was her flesh. A smile crossed his face as he realized the hour. It would be time for evening mass shortly. Tonight's sermon would be on original sin.

❧❧

"I'm blacking out most of the time now. Please tell me what is happening!"

I am trying, Fernanda. These tales are from your ancestors, humans who worshipped me long ago. Their language and vision must be preserved in their tongue. I can feel your friends are close to understanding. I have attempted to touch the one you are closest with in her dreams.

"Is it working?" Fernanda asked.

I do not know. Time will tell. But I will admit, sometimes I forget how your time and aging are different from mine.

"Were you ever human? We don't deal well with things we can't control or see."

I have never been human. Only adored by them. I have seen what the worst impulses are capable of but also envy the bodily experiences you enjoy yet take for granted.

"The things you have taught me. I want to act on them."

With the young man Ruben?

"Yes."

Then if he feels the same, have him with my blessing.

Fernanda could feel the warmth of the goddess receding.

Twelve a.m. glowed red. A shadow crossed Fernanda's open blinds. Ruben stood there with his hand outstretched as he looked side to side. She opened the window wide enough to escape.

"I parked around the corner," he whispered. "My truck makes way too much noise."

Together they ran through the dark. Fernanda's heart beat hard from running but also from knowing what she wanted from Ruben. They sat in the truck without him turning on the ignition.

"Where do you want to go?"

Fernanda placed her hand on Ruben's thigh and then leaned over and kissed him. "Let's go to Espada Park. No one is there and we can have a bit of privacy. I want you all for myself."

They lay in the bed of his truck in the glow of a battery-operated lamp. Ruben had placed blankets on the hard metal. He breathed heavily next to her.

"Do it like this." She guided his hand between her thighs, the way she did to herself.

"You feel so good, Fernanda. I can't believe this is happening," he moaned.

"Kiss me while you touch me," she whispered.

Hungrily he placed his mouth on hers. His erection through his jeans rubbing against her thigh made her want to feel it in her hand. This made her even wetter, the friction from their intertwined fingers even more pleasurable. Round and round, slower and faster, until the sunburst exploded. She could feel Ruben shudder next to her. They both panted hot breath onto each other in their post-orgasm euphoria. Wilted in the best of ways.

"Fuck. I will have to say I spilled a drink in my lap in the drive-through if anyone sees me." They both laughed and held each other.

Fernanda could feel herself drifting off in the dark, his body keeping her warm. "What time is it?"

He lifted his wrist, his face still nuzzled into her neck. "Almost two."

"Shit. Need to get home."

Ruben looked at her with a dreamy expression. "Sure thing."

The drive back was quiet as she laid her head against the glass.

Ruben stopped just before her house. "I want to see you soon. Tomorrow? You know I leave soon, and I want to talk about whatever *this* is." He seemed wide awake and eager.

"I also wanted to know if maybe you would consider coming to England with me. A visit at first. Maybe longer if you like it. I've been thinking about you a lot. You're perfect to me, Fernanda."

"I will let you know." Fernanda reached for the door handle.

"All right. Be careful going inside. I don't want to know what your mom would do to me if she caught us."

The thought of her mother slightly spoiled the joy of the night. He was right, despite the fact that her mother adored Ruben.

"Bye, Ruben." She jumped out of the high cab and ran to her bedroom window.

Damn. Fernanda had made sure to leave it open a crack but now it was closed. It wasn't locked so she could still get in, but the noise might wake her mother. With both palms tucked beneath the ledge she pushed the window up as slowly as possible. No sound. Just a little wider and she would have enough room to slip in. Fernanda put one foot in and then ducked her head beneath the window. As she swung her other leg in, she grazed the corner of her bed. She let out a closed-mouth moan and squeezed her eyes shut. Then footsteps. Her insides trembled; she didn't know what to say or do.

Goddess, I need your help! she silently screamed.

🐖🐖

The light flicked on. Mrs. Garcia held her housecoat closed with one hand. The sound of a revving engine had woken her up. She stood at her bedroom door listening. A thump came from Fernanda's room. Mrs. Garcia ran to her, flinging the door open. There stood her daughter, in front of the open window. She had a long red scrape on her leg.

"What are you doing? It is dangerous out there at night. Did those girls put you up to this? I should have never . . ."

As Mrs. Garcia hurried closer, Fernanda snapped her head towards her mother. But it was not Fernanda. Her eyes glittered bright yellow and green beneath the light. She made a hissing sound.

"El Diablo!" Mrs. Garcia screamed.

Fernanda grabbed her mother's face, bringing it close to her own, and inhaled. Memory sparked like embers and blew into Fernanda's mouth.

Mrs. Garcia could only stand there, feeling particles of her mind and heart float away. It was the one secret she kept. The most difficult. She wanted to cry, but it was done. She hoped whatever was doing this would not tell Fernanda. Anything but that.

Fernanda let her go, and then climbed into bed. Mrs. Garcia could only stand there dumbly, unable to move, just ponder the consequences of the secret that had been taken from her.

Chapter 7

The air conditioner clanked and wheezed, blowing semi-cold air. The sound made the workday seem even longer. You would think with all the frozen drinks we sold they could afford a new unit; then again, they were paying a premium for the water needed to make all that frozen shit. I drank my fill for free, my lips so red from wild cherry slush I didn't even need lipstick.

Mrs. Garcia came in a wet oily mess just like me. I hoped she had looked in the mirror. Without a greeting, she spoke:

"I am afraid of Fernanda and am more afraid for her than ever. She attacked me last night."

Mrs. Garcia melted before my eyes. I had seen my mother like that so many times, even though she did her best to hide it. Suddenly, I felt sorry for her despite the fact that she had never shown an ounce of compassion for me.

It wasn't right, but I took one small jab to let her know not to fuck with me today, not at work, not when I was being watched by my boss for any reason to fire my ass.

"Did you do something to deserve being attacked? Like having another priest try to exorcise her?"

She looked wounded.

"Lourdes, break time!" my manager shouted from the kitchen.

"I will give you five minutes, Mrs. Garcia."

She nodded, and I poured her a large lime slushy because it tasted like a non-alcoholic margarita. If only there was tequila.

"Tell me." I slid the drink to her and walked to the other side of the counter.

"It was about two or three in the morning when I heard noises and went to check on Fernanda. When I switched on the light, she hissed at me. I could see a cut on her leg, so I went to help her. Well, she grabbed my face like she was going to kiss or bite me. I felt my insides twist until something broke. She took something from me, something that has been buried for a long time. I'm ashamed to say it felt good to be rid of it."

Mrs. Garcia clutched the neck of her sweat-soaked blouse and the cross that lay beneath as she drank the slush. "Fernanda might know that she isn't my child.

She is Yolanda's. Yolanda was only fifteen when she got pregnant. She was always the smart one with dreams. I offered to take the baby. We didn't have the same *options* as you girls today. I was married and settled. Pete had a good job with the post office already. The deal was I had full control of raising Fernanda without interference. As time went on, I took it as a blessing from Jesus because Yolanda went on to have more children and a career. Pete and I were never blessed with a child of our own. I will never have another one. She is all I have.

"What do you think we should do? You have been friends for a long time now and probably know her better than me."

All I could do was stare at her dumbly, not knowing if I'd heard her right. This was a bomb of information. My first instinct was to call Fernanda. Had the inhabitant even allowed her this life-altering information? First the possession and now this strange extraction that Fernanda seemed capable of. This was more of a puzzle every day. Without a box cover to reference, we would build in the dark.

"What did she do after?"

Mrs. Garcia sucked down on the slush, flinching at the tartness. "She just kissed me on my forehead and said it was okay with these eyes I can't forget. Reptile eyes! Dios! Then she got into her bed. She is sleeping, I suppose. Her father is at home watching over her. I had to come here to speak to you."

I looked at the clock. What was left of my break would not be long enough to talk to the girls. Should I even tell them? My mind was a hurricane of questions. I needed time to think.

"If anything changes, call me straight away."

Mrs. Garcia smiled and nodded.

"Thank you for the drink. Even though I'm scared for my daughter, I am glad she will know the truth. How to tell her has weighed on me for so long. Yolanda and I have fought over it. Also . . . I know I haven't always been nice to you. I'm sorry. Having this weight off me has made me think about many things."

No one had ever apologized to me for anything in my life. This stunned me as much as her intimate revelation had. "Thank you, Mrs. Garcia. But know I won't take any more abuse again. No more slandering me for no reason. Stop fighting me and listen. Really listen. That is all I want."

She nodded her head and shuffled out. I had a double shift to get through and wouldn't go to Fernanda until the morning.

As if Ana could sense I was about to call her, her name popped up on my phone when I switched it back on after work.

"Hey. I was thinking about you. You will never guess . . . "

"Lourdes! I think I have an idea."

"Tell me!" First Mrs. Garcia apologizing and now an idea from Ana. Either hell was freezing over or our luck was changing.

"I don't know why we didn't do it before, but we need to find someone who speaks Nahuatl. Take them to see Fernanda. I was thinking about that dream of yours. I couldn't stop obsessing over it. It felt *real*."

It was what I had been trying to do on my own, but I was so out of my depth. There had to be someone. This was Texas. "I'm on it."

"Wait. What were you going to tell me?"

I wasn't sure if I should tell Ana Mrs. Garcia's secret before I knew more about Fernanda's condition, plus finding a solution was more important. I wanted to get home and start searching.

"Mrs. Garcia apologized. Look, I am going home now. Let's both look and see where we get."

I sped home, my adrenaline surging. I rushed past my mother and stepfather watching TV and into the room where we had the one computer. I spent the rest of the night trying to find someone local who spoke Nahuatl. UTSA is one of the universities in San

Antonio. The answer could be a scholar. Who else would know, besides someone in Mexico?

I hadn't given my dream a second thought; only part of me wanted to believe in the power of dreams and visions. I'm Mexican—how could I not remember the stories of the campesino, Juan Diego and his vision of La Virgen appearing to him, calling to him to build a shrine and gifting him with her image on his cloak? I've been to the church in Mexico where it is said this happened.

A vision is only as powerful as the will behind it. All else had failed to this point, why not believe a dream? Juan Diego held fast to that dream that became a place of purpose and faith.

I looked up the faculty at UTSA. A professor of Mexican and pre-Columbian history caught my attention, Dr. Camacho. Her office hours were listed as 9 a.m. to 4 p.m. That I had relied on the internet instead of going straight to a real source of information made me feel idiotic and inadequate, not that I needed help in that department. My brain was always tuned to doing things alone, taking charge without help. To ask for help I'd have to brave potential rejection and ridicule.

I would go to her office first thing in the morning. She would be my priest and curandera.

👁👁

I walked down the mostly empty hall of history department offices. A woman not much older than myself mopped the floor at the very end and looked up at the sound of my footsteps. She had the same look as I did behind the till at Sonic. The smell of Pine-Sol burned strong. Something inside of me ached. I wondered what it would be like in a crowd of students, going from class to class. Every room a doorway to an entire universe of knowledge, different subjects with millions of pages written about each one. A hope beyond hope to one day be counted as part of this community.

Footfalls disturbed my thoughts. A woman in her sixties walked down the hall with a large canvas bag slung over her shoulder, her hair a mixture of jet black and white in a single braid down her back. She wore an Emiliano Zapata T-shirt with Mi Tierra printed on the top, jeans, and worn cowboy boots that made a sharp sound that echoed in the hallway. Upon seeing me, she gave me a warm smile, like I was one of her students that she couldn't quite place.

"Hi there. Are you waiting for me?"

"Hello, my name is Lourdes. I'm not a student, but my friend is experiencing something that I don't completely understand. I thought you might since your bio says you speak multiple indigenous languages. I know she wants to communicate with me, however, I just don't have the knowledge. Would you be willing to come see her?"

Her face loosened at this vague request dropped at her feet.

"What do you mean by *experiencing* if it is a language issue?"

I opened my mouth to speak and then closed it again. How could I adequately explain the story without sounding batshit crazy? How would she react to me saying my friend is possessed?

"I'm not trying to sound fresh, but I think it is better if you see for yourself. Please . . . you're our Obi-Wan Kenobi . . . our only hope." My muscles ached with the tension and fear. I hoped she could see the desperation in my eyes. I was not one for begging, but I was not above begging now if I had to.

She now looked at me with concern. "I suppose I could stop by later."

I almost jumped out of my shoes. "Thank you so very much."

I gave her the address and made my way straight to Fernanda's house to inform Mrs. Garcia of my plan. I was nervous to see Fernanda after Mrs. Garcia's confession. I never thought I'd see the day when Mrs. Garcia had no fight inside of her.

When the professor arrived, Fernanda was sitting in the backyard just as she had done every day before. Lately, she'd been lying in her mother's flower beds to masturbate and then fall asleep. If this happened when I was present, I would cover her with a sheet so she might release whatever was inside of her. As her mother and father retreated to the house and turned the TV on loud, I would walk away happy that she was getting some pleasure because it was usually after orgasming and sleep that she was closest to being Fernanda again. Hell, I always felt I could tolerate the world a little more after loving myself.

Earth clung to her hair and between her toes, the dirt between her legs blood-soaked. Her mother hadn't managed to get her to wear a pad that day. The professor sat next to Fernanda, studied her in silence, and then began to speak in Nahuatl. Fernanda's head slowly rolled to the side—part of me almost feared it would turn 360 degrees by the tightening of her mouth into a wide grin. A glimmer of hope and a smile crossed her face, the first in ten days. She opened her mouth and spoke, clear as she would in English or Spanish. The language rolled off her tongue in such a natural way. Every glottal stop, long vowel, and inflection was perfect, as I now know.

Professor Camacho's eyes widened. She looked at me as she pulled out her phone to record the conversation. Relief at last. But what did any of it mean?

After an hour, Fernanda curled up into a ball and fell asleep in the dirt. Mrs. Garcia gave Dr. Camacho a quick hello and returned inside after seeing nothing had changed. We walked to the professor's car in silence. When she knew no one from the house was in earshot, she spoke.

"Your friend is inhabited. I don't want to use the word possessed. Tell me the beginning of all of this?"

I recounted our séance, telling her that I had called for an old spirit.

"Based on what she has said and what I have seen, I think she is inhabited by Tlazoltéotl. She is a fierce goddess; one I believe to be misunderstood but important. She is known as the goddess of filth. She is the eater of sin and the unclean. However, she also represents fertility after death."

"Why the black lipstick? Is this goddess a Goth?"

She shook her head and allowed herself a light chuckle. "As the eater of filth her mouth is surrounded by black. Young women would sometimes smear bitumen around their mouths as they approached womanhood. I believe this is why she is wearing the black makeup. She is expressing all the attributes of this goddess. Blood for her fertility, the black is the sin she consumes, the masturbation because she represents female sexuality, and because the earth is where we come from and where we return in a never-ending cycle."

"Will she be like this forever?"

"The gods of our ancestors were deemed savage and wiped out, much like the people themselves. We know some about them, but much of our knowledge of our ancestors is from the invaders. Their own words are subject to interpretation based upon the remains of their civilization. This goddess must have heard your call and answered. I don't know for sure, but I'm willing to find out. This is a miracle, to hear of the world from one of our own."

"But why us? People call on spirits all over the world. We are just young women."

"Why is anyone called to anything? Maybe Fernanda was just more accessible to the goddess. Something symbiotic between the two. Symbiosis is important in nature; nature has thrived on the concept. I would like to see her again, and I'd like you to come along. I've got some books you might like on ancient ritual and beliefs. Meet me here tomorrow so I can present a plan to her and her mother."

We would meet after work the following day. I needed to tell the others about this breakthrough and I wanted them all there. Together, we would show up at Fernanda's door with the professor.

Thanks to Ana we might be closer to a solution. Fernanda's house tomorrow at 3.

◁▷

Dr. Camacho picked me up so we could drive to Fernanda's together. She wanted to help me save money on gas. I figured it was as good a time as any to tell her about my dreams.

"Do you think the goddess will move to another person after Fernanda?"

She seemed caught off guard by this question.

"I won't know until we get the full story. Why do you ask?"

I recounted my dreams as vividly as I could, trying to remember each detail. Every time I re-read what I wrote about the dream, a new idea would emerge. I hoped Dr. Camacho could enlighten me.

"Let me ask you this, Lourdes. Would you want her to? Maybe this is a way for her to touch you without reaching all the way inside. Continue to write them down. Perhaps she can be a muse for you."

A muse. I had become so discouraged I'd stopped writing, but it is true the goddess had reignited something inside of me that lived beyond the work rota at Sonic and helping out with the family. I'd created my own version of the dreams in the context of a bigger world beyond the city limits. With my notebook and pen, I fought not only for Fernanda, but also myself.

"Thank you. For everything."

Dr. Camacho reached over and patted my hand. "Once I was as young as you and didn't know how I would find a place in the world. I was the first to graduate in my family. It took some time. A lot of hard work and tears. Being a woman, a Mexican woman, was not easy. My biggest hope is that it has made the way for young women like you to achieve what you want."

Dr. Camacho parked the car. Her presence and words made me even more determined.

Mrs. Garcia opened the door. Her first reaction was to give us a look of disapproval, until she met my eyes.

"I guess you want to see Fernanda?"

"We are here to help. I brought help."

"Come in, then. It might do her good to see all of you." With a tired sigh she moved away from the threshold.

We gathered in the living room. "Mrs. Garcia, I'm Dr. Camacho and I believe Fernanda is trying to communicate something to us, not just to her family and friends, but to the world. I'd like to bring her to my home to do a translation."

Dr. Camacho turned to Fernanda to speak in Nahuatl. Fernanda's eyes lit up, then she nodded. Mrs. Garcia looked at the professor like she, too, was possessed.

"So you are saying my daughter is not possessed? What then? Something is talking to her. Like a spirit?"

Before the professor could make this sound scary, I jumped in.

"Yes, that is exactly right. Once we get the message from the spirit, it will leave. Maybe there is some ability in the family you didn't know about."

Mrs. Garcia's eyes widened. "Not that I know of, but maybe on her father's side. I will call the family. I knew Fernanda was special but . . . " She trailed off. I could see her brain turning over what she would say and do.

I nodded. Part of me felt bad for lying and preying upon Mrs. Garcia's faith, but at least it would keep her busy and out of our new mission. I wanted space to try this without interruption.

"We will take good care of her. No witchcraft, just listening. I promise we will have Fernanda back." I regretted making that promise as soon as it escaped my mouth. What if I couldn't make good on it?

Fernanda was already up and walking towards the front door. Mrs. Garcia followed her with the look of a woman willing to travel to the end of the universe to end her torment. "Anything to get my daughter back."

We spent hours at Dr. Camacho's home in the following days, a welcome change from sitting outside. The two-bedroom home was decorated with Diego Rivera and Frida Kahlo prints alongside framed album covers from the '50s, '60s, and '70s. Papier-mâché Catrinas, masks from different parts of the world, and bookcases covered an entire wall. I could see books with her name on the front. My cheeks went hot as I felt myself becoming emotional.

Dr. Camacho sat Fernanda in a leather armchair that matched a two-seater sofa where we made ourselves comfortable.

"Lourdes, for now I will address the goddess and record everything. There isn't much for you to do now but support me and your friend. After, you will help me with the translation. I hope you like to read, because that stack of books by the door is for you to take home."

I knew this was a kind way of saying I would be the third wheel for now. If someone was thirsty, get water. This was fine by me. We were getting somewhere.

"Tlazoltéotl. Tell me what you want to say. Why are you here?"

Fernanda's chin hung towards her chest, her hair covering her face. Upon the name of the goddess being spoken, she raised her head. Caiman eyes rolled in their sockets as they inspected our surroundings, and then fixed themselves upon us. A tear fell from the corner of one of her eyes, followed by another before she opened her mouth to speak. Dr. Camacho pressed record on her phone. Whatever sat before me was Fernanda and the woman in my dreams. Both on the verge of becoming. As Fernanda spoke in Nahuatl, Dr. Camacho translated in English.

"As I told Fernanda in her mind, my nature by birth is sin-eating for others to feel free. My mission is storytelling. I want to say that I no longer want to be seen as crazy or a thing to be forgotten. My existence is more than a bloody dirty rag you cast away every month. I am here because would you not answer a cry for help? I look different, my language is something not everyone understands, but the stories from the past are important. Human history has been one of chaos and in chaos many things become lost. People are subjugated and integrated whether they like it or not. I am here to revive those stories from the source. I have traveled a long way through light and volatile stardust. The stars in the night sky are moth holes in space-time and the bodies of the larvae between each hole are the means of travel.

But here I am. In this place I feel like an indecipherable message in a bottle, but the messages could fill volumes. So many voices, so much blood.

"There are others like me, brothers and sisters of the old world. But the fire within needs fuel and oxygen to thrive and spread. Cataclysmic energy is needed to create change. You are a product of such a thing. I needed to find a way to get out. Her flesh was welcoming and her soul kind, but I cannot leave until my mission is complete.

"I have allowed the girl to taste sin only once, but I have to be careful with how much I show her. Humans are fragile things in mind and ego. In time she will know more. She will grow into a woman as the human life cycle demands.

"What drew me to these females was their love for each other. The strength within each of them to withstand the fires they live with and the fires to come. So many fires you will have to endure if your generation survives. I still do not know if I should show Fernanda the spectrum of time I hold in my hands. I see some of the future shared by others like me, and I hold all of the past memories of their ancestors."

The inhabitant came alive through Fernanda's voice and body. Her story began with cosmic wonders far beyond our reach of this universe. The goddess is from such a place. Before Christ or La Virgen, others existed. A cosmic crash gave birth to this world and soon they all made their way here to see the new creation. It had been an arduous journey because the universes do not reveal their secrets easily; neither do the gods.

She moved on to the tales from our ancestors before colonization. The Olmec, Maya, and Aztec stories in their purest form: tiny embers of inspiration from the original authors that the gods preserved. I sat in a dream-like state, feeling as I did whenever I saw an airplane leave a white streak across the blue Texas sky. Where in all the millions of places was it going, and how I ached to be up there instead of down here. Fernanda's face turned downcast when history changed, and the colonizers arrived. My face, all our faces, wet from the tears of heartache and tragedy.

The stories that intrigued the professor the most were the ones about prophecy, the end. The cycle the earth was experiencing was like the cycle we went through every month, except this was accelerated, unnatural. Humans seemed to be on the brink of self-annihilation.

After a week of nonstop translation, there was a shift. The more stories Fernanda told, the fewer spells she had as the goddess. Fernanda told me she had no memory of the stories, only the conversations she had with the voice in her head.

It was getting closer to when Fernanda was due to start school. Her mother made excuses for her missing orientation.

It was at this time that Perla began her translations into Spanish. New books, our books. The four of us women sat in a circle: Fernanda reciting to Dr. Camacho while I made sense of the stories in English, which I then passed to Perla to translate to Spanish. When Fernanda was not the goddess, she did what she needed to do to prepare for school. We were doing all we could to help her make that deadline. It was good to laugh with our friend again, see her talk about nonsense. Her confidence seemed to soar.

One day, Dr. Camacho surprised me with a question.

"Lourdes. What do you want to do? What are your plans?"

I couldn't remember the last time an adult had asked me that.

"I don't know. I can't do much."

"Mentirosa," Perla casually shot out.

"I'm not a liar. I don't have enough money to do anything."

"Mira, what are you doing now? Remember freshman year when you had to read out that poem in English?"

I remembered. That was why I kept my words away from people I knew. The room went silent, and I felt like an utter fool for thinking the oil and water inside of me made any sense.

"Yeah, no one said a word because I'm an ignorant talentless shit bag."

"Hey, don't talk like that. No one said anything because we were all shocked. I mean it was heavy stuff. Beautiful. Scary as shit. Even if we'd said we liked it you wouldn't have believed any of us. Am I right?"

My face felt hot.

"I hope you are still writing."

I nodded my head, noticing the three of them were looking straight at me. I still did not mention I had a closet full of notebooks. There was probably the same amount of ink on those pages as blood and tears in my body.

Dr. Camacho broke the circle on the table. She handed me an envelope addressed to UTSA.

"Lourdes, when you leave today please put this in the mailbox outside."

It was also this day when, as I drove Fernanda home, she confided in me. With all the windows rolled down, we had to talk loudly.

"Remember you asked me about Ruben?"

I glanced at her and then back at the road. "Yes. You ready to confess?" I joked.

"I've had a crush on him for a long time. At graduation we kissed but it wasn't until the goddess came into my life that I allowed myself to stop thinking that it was sinful and began being less afraid of the future. When I pleasured myself, loved myself as it turns out, those things seemed to matter less and less."

I smiled, happy she could confide in me again.

"And Ruben?"

"I have been sneaking out to see him."

I glanced at her again. "We are women now and we should enjoy what that means to us. It is good to have you back."

Fernanda nodded as the warm wind blew through her hair. Everything felt promising and on the cusp of changing.

Chapter 8

When not fulfilling his church obligations, Father Moreno watched. He watched them with the same fascination as those first statues of La Virgen he was given as a child.

Lourdes was easy because if not at work, she would be at Fernanda's home or at the house of a woman who lived alone. This was advantageous because there would be no man to object to him. The tricky part would be getting Fernanda to the church for the videotaped exorcism. When he took possession of her, she couldn't be that demon that had tried to suck out his soul; it was far too powerful for him and might succeed this time. He needed her to be the accommodating young woman who trusted his authority, or at least whose mother did. Her mother would be the way in. When she was securely tied to a chair, he would draw the thing out, focusing on those unnatural eyes. Letting God's glory shine for all those doubting Thomases.

This had to work because he could no longer sleep. He lay in bed shivering from the cold that would grip him even with all the windows open to let in the sultry night air. Two thick blankets covered his nude body for extra insulation. He slept nude because everything he owned left his skin feeling like it was covered by the bites of a million bees. No matter what he did, the tundra remained. By morning his sheets were soaked with sweat. Perhaps the demon was tormenting him, knowing its days were numbered. However, he had felt this before—right after he laid Martha to rest in the freezer.

As he approached the home of Mrs. Garcia, he straightened his collar, which was strangling him. The doorbell rang inside the house, and it wasn't long before he could hear the inside lock click. He lifted the bag of pan dulce for her to see.

"Good afternoon, Mrs. Garcia. Do you have time for a coffee and something sweet?" The weariness and deep purple shadows beneath her eyes told him she would let him in.

"Oh, yes. Come in. Fernanda is resting. I would love some company." She unhooked the screen door.

🐝🐝

Fernanda left her bedroom door ajar so she could hear her mother's conversation with the priest. Only parts were audible, so she stepped out in the hallway.

"But Father, she is getting better! It is a miracle. The spirit is going."

Fernanda took another step to hear more. She wanted to know what this priest was thinking and why he was back. The goddess had said that he couldn't be trusted and something about him made her feel this, too. He was speaking just loud enough for her to hear.

"Witchcraft. It could be a demon, Mrs. Garcia. Can you really trust her friend Lourdes or that professor? I have seen her books. They are about pagan beliefs. Old ways before the church. You need to be careful. How much do you really know? Just what they tell you?"

"I will keep an eye out, Father. Thank you."

"That is what I am here for. You know where to find me."

When Fernanda heard him say goodbye, she slipped back into her room as quietly as possible, inching the door closed to prevent the sound of the click. Flashes of memory made her head throb. The voice in her head spoke.

Fernanda, listen to me. Be careful around that man. I may have many powers; however, I cannot control those who are not willing. He is unpredictable. He seems to be, as you call it, possessed by his faith.

The voice paused.

Also, if you want me to leave you, I will.

Fernanda faced the window, her back to the door. Through the slits of the blinds she could see Father Moreno looking at their house, taking photos. He was an odd man.

"No. I don't want you to go. Where would you go?"

I would try another host, but I have been searching and waiting for the right human and the right time. I have tried this before with others but none were as willing to host me as you.

"I will do as you say, but I know you are keeping things from me. I feel like I'm going crazy. Please let me in. I want to know what you know.

Tlazoltéotl was silent. *Very well. I will start with the things at hand. What you need to know about what is happening in this time and place. Then I will show you the stories I have been telling through your voice in your dreams. When you sleep tonight, I will begin.*

Fernanda was satisfied with that. Having a mind split in two would eventually drive her to the brink of sanity.

"One more thing. I can understand you, but the others can't. Why is this?"

You understand me because I am inside of you. We are as one. And what I need them to hear should be pure. I want the stories heard in the original tongue. They come from your mouth as if you were me. That is why neither you nor they understand.

"I trust you, my friend. When will I stop feeling totally afraid and be strong like you?"

Allowing your fear to deter you is the only thing that should frighten you. You have a lot of power, Fernanda.

Fernanda glanced in her mirror and saw the caiman eyes of Tlazoltéotl, the sister she never had.

"You know, I think I love him. Ruben and I are so much alike, and he says he loves me, but I love myself more. I don't want to give up my dreams and move to England."

It's okay, Fernanda. It is natural to love, to touch. To touch without love and experience the pleasures given to us is also fine.

"Tlazoltéotl. If I promised you my soul, would you help me succeed? I want to make my family proud. My friends all think I'm invincible and perfect. I just don't want to let anyone down, and I'm so scared that I will. You can have my soul in exchange for this."

The goddess was silent again.

My dear, I do not deal in the currency of souls. That is another god that I do not cross paths with. Besides, humans have this belief that the soul is theirs to give. It is not. It is part of something you could not even comprehend, and even as a goddess I would struggle to explain. I am part of it, too; however, I come from someplace very different. And you are already on a path to be successful in your own right. Don't allow your self-doubt or fear to be stumbling blocks. You will find your success in being fearless.

"If you stay, will you just be a voice in my head?"

Yes and no. I would work through you. I told you I am here to eat sin, to tell the world stories from our ancestors, to give humans hope and reveal secrets from where I am from. All of this combined, like your friendships, is to prepare you all for the next phase of this world. Together, we would walk through the fires.

The truck waited for her as arranged. Fernanda could feel herself shaking inside, but that wasn't distracting her. It was the ache, the wetness between her legs, the anticipation of what was about to happen. How good it was in her mind and every time they were together. Fernanda told the goddess to sleep that night. She wanted to be alone with Ruben, her first full sexual experience with a man.

She slipped out the window, looking both ways before dashing in the dark to the passenger side of the truck. Ruben looked so good. He smelled of a hint of cologne, sage and tobacco. Fernanda smiled, knowing he didn't know that tonight she wanted to fuck him. His body inside of hers.

"You want to go to the same place? I think of it as our spot now."

"You know I do."

The streets were dark with a sheen of moonlight. The park was deserted. When he brought the truck to a stop, he left the radio on, tuned to an oldies station.

"Push your seat back."

Ruben looked at her and half smiled. "This is new. Okay."

Fernanda kicked off her flip flops and straddled Ruben. She brought her lips to his, the soft flesh she wanted more of. She wore nothing underneath her cotton slip dress that tied at the shoulder. She grabbed his hands, placing them on her waist underneath the dress so he could feel that nothing stood between them.

"Fernanda, are you sure? We have never . . . "

"We have never because I wasn't ready and last time . . . just touch me. Kiss me."

She fumbled with the button and zipper of his jeans, then reached into her bag for a condom Lourdes had given her. That girl always had condoms in her purse. Her hands reached into his boxer shorts feeling his cock was hard but the skin soft, like his lips. His lower body tensed at her touch. Watching his excitement excited her. With the condom on she let him slide inside. She bit her lip with the initial pressure, until she gave in like she did with his fingers. The pain subsided. She pulled off her dress so he could see all of her. Their black pubic hair one soft puff of fur. She loved how the moisture of sex felt against her thighs the more she grinded and rolled her hips, his hard cock teasing her clit with delicious licks, like devouring a popsicle before it has a chance to melt in the hot summer sun. Without needing to think, she rocked her body back and forth, relaxing her shoulders, her mind only focusing on Ruben and her pleasure.

Ruben drove her home with one hand holding hers and a smile on his face. D'Angelo's "How Does it Feel" played quietly. When they came to a stop he leaned over to kiss her.

She knew she would have to break his heart, but not tonight, and she kissed him back.

"Goodnight," she said before running from the truck back to her window.

Fernanda lay in bed, feeling a surge of confidence in her body.

"You awake?"

I never sleep, just drift away. Did you enjoy yourself?

"It was better than I expected, but that is why I chose Ruben. I knew he would be kind and loving. Thank you for helping me to feel aware of my body, what it can do. The miracle of it, really."

It is nothing but a natural ability. Goodnight, dear Fernanda.

❧❧

Father Moreno drove back to the church with a sense of accomplishment, the air conditioner on full blast to dry the sweat covering his body beneath his clerical clothing. A feverish chill ran through his backbone, the cold so deep his vertebrae felt like they would fuse together in a permafrost. As he sat across from Mrs. Garcia he couldn't help but glance over her shoulder at the photos of Fernanda. How beautiful she was; he wanted more than anything to restore her purity. The thing he saw before was not her. He would get rid of it and then keep whatever was left of Fernanda. After recording what he needed to prove the existence of demons, he would say she ran away. How could anyone think differently after her rebellious behavior all summer?

When he arrived at the church, the feeling of unwellness was worse than before. Usually he would sit in the confessional to gather his thoughts but today he wanted to be close to Martha. He sat behind his desk with hands clasped in prayer, trying to fight impure thoughts of cold flesh upon his, of ice crystals on her tongue for him to ingest like a host. He fantasized about this being the elixir that would cure him. These blasphemous thoughts were too tantalizing and easy to entertain. The collar around his neck felt noose-tight again. The church-issued clothing needed to come off before it stitched into his skin. Father Moreno jumped from his seat, frantically clawing at the seams of his clothing, pulling at the buttons until they popped off and the loose threads unraveled to what they really were, weak little spindly things. He stood before his collection of La Virgen statues panting from the exertion, all of his clothing torn rags on the floor. They stared back at his nudity. All his life they were enough, sustained him. She was woman perfected as she gave forth life but remained pure. Her life was a sacrifice to her son, the savior.

Now she looked like a cheap copy in plastic and ceramic. Her presence made him sick. Next to the filing cabinet was a faded piñata stick. He gripped it in one hand, lifting it above his head to swing at these women with smug smiles on their faces. Those empty eyes would no longer see him, mock him. His arms thrashed in all directions. The fallen ones he continued to pulverise.

His arms began to ache. On the floor lay a pink cheek and single eye from one of the larger statues. With his bare foot he stood on the ceramic shard until it broke in half. The remaining pieces cut into his skin; a large triangular fragment lodged in the soft arch of his foot.

He pressed it in deeper, allowing it to enter his flesh. The rage slowly subsided.

He had to take Fernanda. Quickly he got dressed and drove back to the Garcia house, where he saw Fernanda climbing out of her window. For a moment he thought it might be the chance to take her, but she was not alone. As she ran from her home, a black truck pulled up to the curb. He knew that truck. It was Ruben's. He followed the vehicle to the edge of Espada Park, the place of missions and ghost stories. Beneath the moonlight, far enough not to be noticed but close enough to see, he stood against the outer wall of the missions in shadow. He clutched the vial of blood at his neck, wet with sweat. His chest remained tight. It couldn't be the girl doing these things; it had to be the demon inside of her. A seducer of men and possessor of virgins. He would have her, too, wrapped in cloth, rosary in hand. Cold and beautiful like his Martha. Her body would be his forever, icy and pure.

When they drove off, he returned to his car, wanting to relieve himself of desire but knowing it would only give the demon what it wanted. He needed God on his side. Father Moreno fished a rosary out of his pocket, pressing the sharp edge into the side of his thigh. A gasp escaped his lips as did the name, *Fernanda*.

Chapter 9

"It's so damn hot out there. I swear we are all going to melt into a puddle of skin and blood, like a raspa cone."

Dr. Camacho looked up from her computer. "I have some drinks in the garage."

"Beer?" Perla asked with a grin.

"You ladies are not twenty-one yet. Bottles of iced tea and sodas."

"I'll get them," Fernanda offered.

"Just through the kitchen, that door leads to the garage."

The doorbell rang.

"I'm not expecting anyone other than Lourdes. She knows to let herself in." Fernanda heard Dr. Camacho get up and open the door.

"I'm sorry to disturb you, but I'm here to take Fernanda home. Her mother sent me."

"I know nothing of this."

"Well, I just came back from seeing Mrs. Garcia. It is urgent."

Fernanda stood at the door between the garage and the kitchen, staring at an unshaven, sweaty Father Moreno. He looked like a man who had walked out of the cold storage of a morgue.

"Liar."

He snapped his head towards Fernanda, startled at the sound of her voice. "I promise you. Your mother needs you now."

"Liar. Go away."

Dr. Camacho gave Father Moreno a smile. "As you can see, Fernanda can speak for herself, and she doesn't want to go with you. You should leave. She is perfectly capable of getting herself home."

Without warning Father Moreno shoved a small pistol into Dr. Camacho's abdomen. The crack of the gun made Perla and Fernanda leap.

"Motherfucker!" Perla lunged towards the priest. He shot the gun twice in Perla's direction, hitting her in the arm and leg.

"Run, Fernanda!" she managed to gasp as she held onto the back of the dining chair. Father Moreno raised the gun to Perla's head.

Fernanda dropped the drinks to the floor. "I'll come with you. Leave her."

Father Moreno turned to Perla.

"Give me your phone, girl!"

Perla was shivering.

"Bag. There." She cocked her head towards the sofa before her legs buckled. Father Moreno looked back at two handbags on the cushion and leaned down to grab both, gun still on Perla.

Fernanda and Father Moreno walked out of the house together and into his car. Fernanda didn't look at Perla or Dr. Camacho because otherwise she might try to kill the priest, or she might break down.

◑◐

I couldn't wait to get to Dr. Camacho's house. The plan was to order Chinese, do a few hours of translation and then watch a movie on pay-per-view. Since we first began our project, Fernanda was living as herself most of the time. Whatever we were doing seemed to be working. I also felt filled with confidence and more hope than I had felt in a long time. The goddess wanted to speak after lying dormant for so long, and so did I. Silence is a bad habit, easy to slip into. I had done it myself. But as of late that had changed. There would be no going back.

I pulled into Professor Camacho's drive, next to Perla's car. This was strange as I swore she'd mentioned a date that night. I walked in without knocking because the professor made this feel like a second home for us, for me. Even when Fernanda was not there, we would still share meals and discuss all the revelations from the goddess. We believed once the stories were put together in their entirety they would reveal something life changing, for everyone.

Perla was on the floor propped against a dining chair clutching her thigh and arm, her skin devoid of color. Dr. Camacho lay in a pool of her own blood, eyes wide open. My body, my heart, disintegrated in that moment. I didn't need to touch the professor to know she was gone. I took out my phone and called an ambulance. Perla moaned. I ran to her.

"Perla! Who did this?"

She was weak, her white lips barely able to move. "Priest. Moreno. Go. Fucking go." I looked from her to Dr. Camacho and then back.

"I can't leave you!"

"Fucking cops will have questions; it will be too late. He will kill her." I couldn't ignore the flaring of Perla's eyes, that female rage we are told to bury when it burns too bright or becomes distracting. Tears filled her bottom lids and then spilled over. "It's going to be okay. Go."

I knew exactly where I was going next. When I started my car, I could hear sirens and then the flashing lights of an ambulance. There was a wave of relief over the grief I had no time to feel.

The rumbling sky looked as if it was about to crack open to unleash some great terror. You could smell the impending moisture; perhaps the time for waters to break had come. Maybe the darkness of space would descend upon us. Lightning and thunder rolled within the clouds. Every car had their headlights on, blinding me more than I already was in my confusion. I had to think fast. My stepfather had a gun in a pocket in the backseat of his truck, but I didn't know how to use it or even if there were bullets inside, and anyway if I wasted another second getting to Fernanda and Father Moreno it might be too late. With the goddess not making as many appearances lately, I wasn't sure if she would protect Fernanda. Or what if the goddess did appear and killed the priest before I got to them? Fernanda would be blamed, her future forever marred.

The only plan I had my mind set on was killing this priest if it came down to us or him. I'd be hated forever. I would take the sin, accept hatred or death. I didn't want to die, but I didn't want Father Moreno or anyone like him to have the satisfaction of our tears or bodies. No, I wanted to strike like a predator in the wild.

The church sat on the corner of the street like a chipped headstone. It appeared rotten, choked by time and its own tangled intolerance. I parked hastily, not caring if I got a ticket, and then ran inside. The vestibule was quiet, but as I moved through the freezing church, I could hear voices in the back rooms. The office was upturned, the temperature far hotter than the rest of the church with the air-conditioning turned off. Broken pieces of statues were strewn across the floor. I couldn't walk without stepping on parts of them.

The priest was shouting something from the Bible over the sound of laughter, the laughter of the goddess. I peered into the adjoining room, not making a sound. I had seen what she was capable of. Fernanda sat on a chair with her hands on her lap. Father Moreno stood before her with a camera propped on a tripod behind him. Bible in one hand and gun in the other.

"Why do you mock me? You are a vile temptation, you have no place here or inside this young woman, making her do things she doesn't want to do. Show yourself! Show everyone what you are. Evil exists!" He tossed water from a plastic flask over her in the shape of a cross.

She laughed harder, louder. "Stop! It burns!"

He moved closer, flustered by her show of defiance. She continued laughing in his face as the water splashed across her body.

"Tell me your name, demon!"

The laughter stopped. A deep voice issued from her lips. "I am not a demon! Stop calling me that." Her eyes flickered with animosity.

"Enough games!" the priest shouted.

"I agree, enough games. Now priest, you will confess *your* sin."

His confidence turned to terror. It knew.

"I am not the sinner! Everything I have done is for the glory of God. You will see, all will see!"

Fernanda crept closer to him one step at a time causing the priest to back into the freezer, the gun outstretched in his trembling hand. I stepped out from the office.

"The police know it is you. It's over."

Against the freezer he waved the gun from Fernanda to me. His demeanor changed. "You won't leave this place. I will kill you both."

The freezer snapped open, bouncing off the wall with a loud thud. The sudden noise caused him to drop the gun. He looked back, then scrambled to the floor to pick up the gun again.

"Let's go, Fernanda! Now's our chance!"

She stared at the freezer with caiman eyes and a wicked smile, her body frozen. Father Moreno rose slowly pointing the gun towards us again.

Crunching. Shifting. Something moved in the freezer. A bluish-white hand with chipped red nail polish and a spider web tattoo between her thumb and index finger lifted the lid. I blinked, not wanting to believe what I was seeing. However, after meeting the goddess, anything was possible. After the hand, a torso lifted up from inside the cold coffin, followed by the head of a woman. Her features were icy white tinged with purple-blue like a Lladró figure. Her wide eyes, polar ice caps, cracked and shifted as they adjusted to the light. They radiated enmity and heartache. My brain registered the sight in slow motion. I still wasn't sure it was real until I glanced at Fernanda. Her lips were pulled back tightly against her face, showing all of her teeth. Flames in her eyes concentrated on the frozen woman with blowtorch intensity. This was Tlazoltéotl at work.

As Father Moreno reared his head to the sounds behind him, the woman in the freezer ripped the mantilla off her head and the robe off her body, revealing a red lace bra. The frozen woman reached for Father Moreno, and with both her hands gripped the sides of his skull. The longer Fernanda stared at the freezer, the more animated the woman became. She opened her mouth, sliding her tongue back and forth across her teeth. Water drained from her body. The priest was paralyzed in her death grip, and the gun slid from his hand. She placed a wet cheek against his rigid face.

"You have robbed me. You have robbed my children. And all you can speak of is God. You want to know of God? Let me show you!" she growled.

The priest's body jerked and spasmed in her grasp. He wailed in such torment I almost couldn't bear the sound. Father Moreno was no longer on this plane; he was somewhere else. In his agony, he screamed "Martha!"

Full blue lips opened, releasing frozen breath that shook in laughter. Black fingertips pressed hard into his skull before releasing him.

Her gaze moved to us. For a moment I thought she would climb out to attack. Instead she raised a hand, reaching out, water dripping from her fingertips.

"Tell them I love them."

The life behind her eyes fled and her body went limp, falling back into the freezer. My brain still struggled to understand. I looked dumbly at Fernanda who was no longer grinning. Tears rolled down her cheeks. I shook her, knowing it wasn't Fernanda.

"Tlazoltéotl, I know you can hear me, and I know it is you. We have been together long enough now I can sense when you are near. I can feel you. You have to let her go. There are rules here, maybe not where you come from, but we have to live by the fucking rules, or we get nowhere. You hear me?" I squeezed the sides of her arms tighter to get a reaction. It was a dummy smile with eyes you would see on a stuffed animal.

"You want this world to accept you and listen to you? You want to own this world? Then play the damn game that humans have to play if you plan on being in one of our bodies. We can't go around doing shit like this. The world has changed. Surely you see this. Think of your mission!" I breathed heavily, not knowing if the priest would wake up any minute, but I didn't break eye contact. I needed to get through to her.

The light that was Fernanda looked back at me. "She said you are right."

Fernanda threw her arms around me, and I held onto her. Father Moreno lay on his back staring at the ceiling, his chest rising and falling quickly with erratic breathing. He wasn't going anywhere. I dialed 911, said as little as possible, and then gave my phone to Fernanda to call her parents. It was over.

We walked out of the church to a downpour. A thick fog steamed the streets, blurring the street lights and headlights. Fernanda and I clung to each other in the cold. We didn't want to go back inside. We heard the police and ambulance before we saw them through the fog. The ambulance took Father Moreno away. He was still alive, but unresponsive. Only time would tell if he would awaken to confess the truth.

Mr. and Mrs. Garcia arrived at the church. Both jumped out of their car in tears as they embraced their daughter. "Mija! What happened?"

Fernanda pulled away from her parents but placed a hand on her mother's cheek.

"Mamá, I want to see Yolanda."

Mrs. Garcia's eyes wobbled with pooling tears. She kissed Fernanda's hands and nodded without saying a word. The three of them gathered close again. Her eyes looked up at me as I stood there shivering, holding my arms. "Thank you," she mouthed.

I nodded and moved to the side waiting for the cops to question me, ask me what I did to the priest. I also wanted to alert them to the body in the freezer. Someone out there wanted to know where she was, whoever she was. She also proved Father Moreno was not a good man. It might have been us in another freezer. The cops insisted on escorting me home to make sure I was okay. I doubted that was the reason. My family's hugs felt plastic.

I went straight to bed to message my friends for a meeting the next day. It would be all over the news by then. I needed a plan for the worst-case scenario of my ass getting blamed. Father Moreno had to wake up.

Two days later I was informed that Father Moreno had a brain aneurysm, but he would survive. They had determined I was telling the truth and no further action would be taken. It was also at this time that his secret was revealed. Martha had been missing for over a year. Everyone assumed she abandoned her children for a lover because of a note left in her car in the parking lot of the Target she frequented. All her belongings were found in the priest's home neatly folded or hanging next to his own clothes. Even her shoes sat next to his. An album with photos ranging from their childhood up to the point she went missing lay next to his bed. She'd died from a head trauma, but there had been no sexual assault. Her body would be given a proper burial so her family could mourn their loss and her children would know she didn't leave them.

Father Moreno remained in the hospital for weeks as they tried to determine how to treat him. He wasn't well enough for prison or to stand trial for the murder of Martha Sanchez. As he became increasingly incoherent and disoriented, speaking in Latin and delivering sermons to himself, he was transferred to a psychiatric ward for the remainder of his life.

Chapter 10

Fernanda stood at the farthest edge of Military Highway before it meets the freeway and undeveloped land. The moon was a bitten-off fingernail with only the faintest light illuminating the darkness. She breathed heavily, waiting. A single car approached, shining two lights on her, the engine still running. Her head hung toward her chin, her arms straight against her legs.

The car door opened. "You all right there, miss? Are you hurt? Can we escort you home?" A woman stepped out of the car. She held a cloth with chloroform in her hand behind her back.

Fernanda didn't move or make a sound until the woman stood close enough for her to grab the woman's head with both hands. Caiman eyes bulged with fury, her mouth opening wide to release the bulbous tongue ready to eat the woman's sin.

The woman's hand clenched as she tried to fight the strength within Fernanda.

"Tell me your sin," Fernanda hissed.

"No!" screamed the woman as she tried to bring the cloth to Fernanda's nose. Another car door opened, and a man with a Dallas Cowboys hat ran toward them. He stopped when Fernanda began sucking a black vapor from his girlfriend's mouth.

The woman convulsed violently, her body burning from the inside out, beginning at the scalp line, then spreading to the rest of her body until it blackened to a charred thing. The smell of burnt flesh rose into the atmosphere, clinging to the still air. Flakes of flesh blew into the cool autumn breeze. The man doubled over to vomit. Fernanda dropped the corpse and began to calmly walk to the man. He looked up from the ground, chunks of food and strings of bile falling from his lips.

"Confess," Fernanda whispered.

He pulled a Taser from behind his back. "I don't know what you are, but I'm going to give it to you now, you ugly bitch!" He switched it on, lunging towards Fernanda.

She grabbed his hand, breaking it at the wrist. His scream drowned out the sound of the cracking of bones. As he looked at his broken wrist in terror, Fernanda shoved the Taser and his hand into his mouth. He fell to the ground as the Taser sent jolts of electric currents through his body. His forehead singed beneath the cap, smoke rising as the black continued down his body until it, too, was a burnt carcass.

Fernanda walked back the way she came. It would be a long distance, but she had Tlazoltéotl to keep her company.

"Should we call the police?" Fernanda whispered, a hint of cloud escaping her lips as she spoke.

I don't want to. Do you?

Fernanda continued to walk at a calm pace. "It will be dawn soon. There will be enough traffic; they will be found. But it makes me sad."

Do you feel remorse?

"I am sad because there are so many other sinners like that out there. Like the stars, doing bad things that are only seen long after the deed is done."

Don't worry, Fernanda. We will continue to bring justice, though not like this. Humans have created a system to process wrongdoing, to weed out the guilty and innocent. It is imperfect, but it is all you have. You can lead the way for change. Bring a real sense of equality and justice in the way humans need. Look at how big the night sky is. That should be your ambition.

Fernanda stopped and looked above her head. The sky didn't end.

"You are right. Let us work together. And I like the idea of making it official one day."

Fernanda could hear the TV volume higher than usual

that morning when she walked out of her bedroom. Her mother turned to her. "Mija, listen."

If you are just joining us, here are the headlines. Father Moreno, the man convicted of the murder of Martha Sanchez, has been moved to a psychiatric facility where he will serve his sentence. It is unknown if this was a single incident or if there are other victims.

Another tragedy unfolding is the raiding of a trafficking ring led by Paul and Corinne Maddox. It also appears they have murdered young men and women, whose bones were found in their home. Ten children kidnapped at the border and South Texas have been taken into care. The couple's involvement was only discovered after their bodies were found outside their car off Military Highway. It appears they were set alight. We will keep you updated on this case.

And now to Damien Pierce for the weather.

Well, folks, it looks like our prayers have been answered and we are expecting thunderstorms throughout the week. This couldn't come at a better time because the reservoir is at dangerous levels. Flooding alerts are expected to be issued.

👁👁

The letter I posted for the professor was a recommendation for a scholarship for entrance to her department and a paid work-study under her. I cried for days after receiving this news, the image of her body in my mind entangled with a feeling of overwhelming gratitude.

The university respected the professor's wishes and I was admitted with a full scholarship as long as I kept my grades above a 3.5 GPA. I thanked the heavens for this gift and wasn't about to fuck it up. On the weekends I made sure to visit Dr. Camacho's grave. Beneath the auburn trees that signaled the change of season and the welcomed cooler weather, I grieved for her. It was also time for my interview with the history department to see if I could keep my work-study and continue deciphering the stories.

Pauline accompanied me, ready to stand by my side if needed. My body was a live wire, the fear threatening to make my legs run away. But I could do this.

"You ready?"

I looked at the cover page of the first translations with Dr. Camacho's name next to mine and Perla's. "Yeah, as ready as I will ever be. I promise Dr. Camacho will never be forgotten. Tlazoltéotl and all her knowledge will be in the world."

"If anyone says you can't hold a dream in your hands, you can show them that. No one can take it away."

"Don't make me cry, Pauline! Not now."

We giggled like we were back in school sharing gossip. We were women, finding our way in a world that didn't give us a second glance.

"No! I'm sorry. Don't cry. Find that strength you have shown all this time. I know it's there. You go in there and kick some ass. Don't curse. And after we'll go get some Whataburger. My treat."

"I better not fuck up then."

The door to the conference room opened.

"We are ready for your presentation."

Pauline and I looked at each other with wide eyes and smiles. She gave me an assuring nod before I turned to follow the department head through the door that changed the course of my life.

After three weeks I learned the work-study was approved. I thanked the goddess in my mind for her blessing of the stories. We didn't know what the future would look like for any of us, only that it was ours.

🐛🐛

Fernanda started college as planned. She sent us regular updates about her classes and new friends. She decided to run for student government, something she was asked to do many times in high school by various teachers but had always declined, claiming she didn't have enough time with her school work. Now she made the time. This was the beginning of a Fernanda who seemed happy and enthusiastic about her future. It would be okay.

Whatever worries she harbored the year before were all but gone. Her self-assuredness blossomed.

Tlazoltéotl remained in hibernation, only coming out when she was called by Fernanda. There she worked through her, with her; they listened to each other in harmony, achieving their goals with the help of the other.

The night before Fernanda left, we sat in a circle on my floor with a bottle of tequila. Depeche Mode played low on my stereo. We looked at each other, remembering the night it all began.

Fernanda broke the silence. "Thank you for always being by my side. I know it was frightening and had an ugly end. I wish to God it did not happen the way it did. If only Dr. Camacho's death could have been prevented. But we stuck together. To being Chicana brujas always."

She raised her shot of tequila with tears in her eyes and pupils vibrating. Tlazoltéotl was with us.

"And to the goddess for her teachings. May her words show us the way." I raised my shot.

"To Dr. Camacho," said Ana.

Pauline and Perla looked at each other. "To us."

With tears streaming down our cheeks, we necked the smooth and smoky alcohol and then turned on *The Craft* one last time.

V. CASTRO is a Mexican American author from San Antonio, Texas now residing in the UK. She is a full-time mother, a Latinx literary advocate, and co-founder of Fright Girl Summer, a platform to amplify marginalized voices. She writes Latinx novels of horror, erotic horror, and science fiction, including her most recent, *Hairspray and Switchblades*. Connect with Violet via Instagram and Twitter @vlatinalondon or at www.vvcastro.com.

CREATURE PUBLISHING was founded on a passion for feminist discourse and horror's potential for social commentary and catharsis. Seeking to address the gender imbalance and lack of diversity traditionally found in the horror genre, Creature is a platform for stories which challenge the status quo. Our definition of feminist horror, broad and inclusive, expands the scope of what horror can be and who can make it.